The Secret of the Lilies

A.J. Avila

Copyright 2024 A. J. Avila
All Rights Reserved
First edition 2024
This is a work of fiction. Names, characters, places, and incidents are products of the author's imagination or are used fictitiously. This book is licensed for your personal enjoyment only. The scanning, uploading, and distributing of this book via the internet or any other means without the permission of the copyright owner is illegal and punishable by law. Please purchase only authorized editions, and do not participate in or encourage piracy of copyrighted materials. Your support of the author's rights is greatly appreciated.

All scripture quotations are taken from the public domain Douay-Rheims 1899 American Edition

Acknowledgements

A special thank you to Amy Bennett, Jennifer Calgaro, Dianne Fisk, Chris Green, and Sue McDonough.

Dedication

For my Lord and Savior, Jesus Christ
May I spend eternity burning with love for You

Read This First

Many of the incidents in this book are based on someone's true-life experiences. So, if you think a parent would consider a perfect report card not good enough, well, you never met my dad.

Oh, and I actually did have a library card when I was three.

Part I

Markette

And the light shineth in darkness, and the darkness did not comprehend it.

John 1:5

And we know that to them that love God, all things work together unto good, to such as, according to his purpose, are called to be saints.

Romans 8:28

Prologue

I died when I was fourteen years old.

Wait, wait, wait! Do not toss this book aside or delete it off your device!

This is not one of those sappy stories in which a child oh so bravely faces a fatal illness and everybody boo-hoos when she dies.

It's not like that. I promise.

No, really! I promise!

Okay, there is a person in this book who dies that way, but since that's not what my story is about, I'm only going to mention it briefly, later on.

I hope you won't mind if I speak directly to you, the reader. After all, I am writing this to you from beyond the grave.

Allow me to introduce myself. My name is Markette Maria Mason. That's pronounced Mark-ette, with the accent on the second syllable. It's not like the word *market* in supermarket, where the accent is on the first syllable.

It's a rare name, and the reason I got it was because my parents wanted a boy. They were going to name him Mark after my Dad's Uncle Mark. Their reasoning was that, since Uncle Mark was an unmarried multi-millionaire with my father as his only living relative, he might look favorably on Dad in his will if he gave him a namesake instead of leaving all that lovely money to the many charities he normally endowed. But when I came along instead—surprise!—my folks feminized *Mark* by adding *ette*, and voila! I was Markette.

And you know what? Their strategy worked. My great-uncle Mark was tickled pink that I was named after him, especially since I'm a girl. In fact, back in the 1950s, when boys were valued more than girls, he was actually delighted I was a girl. "When you get a boy," he'd said, "you get a buddy. But when you get a girl, you get a princess!"

Although he was a real estate mogul who lived in New York and we lived in southern California, he kept in touch, occasionally flying out to visit and often helping with some of my expenses. And he always called me "princess."

It just occurred to me you may be wondering how I can write this if I'm already dead. Let me put it to you this way: nothing is impossible for God. This also explains why you'll notice I have a vocabulary far beyond the norm for a fourteen-year-old. That's because in Heaven we communicate simply by thought, and those thoughts are being translated into a language you can read.

Oh, and I should also let you know that we in Heaven are aware of doings on Earth. You may have been told we know nothing about such things, but it's in the Bible. There's a verse in the Book of Revelation—Revelation 6:10, to be exact—in which some martyrs ask why their deaths have not yet been avenged. Well, how could they know those deaths weren't avenged if they had no knowledge of what was going on in your world? Then too, there's that bit in Luke 15:10 about angels rejoicing over the repentance of a sinner, and I have to tell you, boy do they rejoice! If you ask them why they're celebrating, they don't say, "Sorry, you're not allowed to know what's happening on Earth." No, they are delighted to share the good news and have us celebrate with them!

That knowledge isn't ours through any power of our own. Oh no! It's through our unity in Christ. He is the vine, and we are the branches, and any branch that hasn't been cut off is still connected. Even death cannot separate us from His love.

Anyway, the first part of this story is about my short life, how I died, and what it was like to encounter God after I died.

You might find that last part incredibly fascinating.

1

My life drastically changed, and not for the better, one hot summer day of 1959 in the home of my mother's best friend from high school, Evelyn Hansen.

Mrs. Hansen had a daughter, Scarlet, right about my age. I didn't know *Scarlet* was an unusual name. To me it was just her name. Maybe her parents gave it to her because she had flaming red hair like her mother. Maybe Mrs. Hansen was a big fan of *Gone with the Wind*.

A blonde neighbor girl, Verna, was also visiting, and we three five-year-olds played with our baby dolls on the beige carpeted living room floor. Scarlet's house was huge. Both of the bedrooms at my home could probably fit into this one space alone. Her place, thankfully, also had air conditioning which hummed in the background as we girls set about the serious business of mothering our babies.

Scarlet's home had two tables to eat at: a kitchen table and an oaken dining room table. The latter was long and could seat a dozen people. Since there were only three persons in Scarlet's family, it probably was used only for special occasions. At the moment it had three large vases of lilies decorating it. Two of the vases, those on the ends, held pure white blossoms. The one in the middle, however, had blood-red flowers. Their fragrance wafted into the living room, and I loved their sweet scent each time I drew in a deep breath.

Frankly, I thought it was rather silly to have two tables when only one could be used at a time. We had just the one gray Formica kitchen table at our house, and I figured that was plenty. But Scarlet's father was a doctor, a surgeon, while my father was a self-employed plumber who only got paid by the job. So we lived on far less. At the time we three girls cared nothing about that. It didn't make one whit of difference to me that Scarlet's house had a swimming pool and ours didn't. Little kids don't notice any disparity between social classes until it gets pointed out to them.

Well, okay, I did wish our house had stairs like Scarlet's did. What fun to go up and down stairs, especially up where I could get a greater view at the top than my three-foot high frame would normally allow. I'd asked my parents if we could install some stairs at our place, and for some strange reason they'd found that laughable.

All our mothers and another lady were at the kitchen table, occupied with a game of bridge and yakking about boring grown-up stuff which I was very happy to mentally tune out.

I glanced in the direction of their gossip. *Why do they want to play with cards?* I wondered. *Grown-ups have all the money! Why don't they buy toys and play with them?*

I shook my head. Grown-ups, I concluded, were not very smart. Nope, children were much smarter.

I considered myself lucky to have my doll. She'd been a gift that had come in the mail from

Great-uncle Mark. I was glad he'd gotten a doll that had brown hair like I did instead of the more popular blonde ones of the time.

I laid her down, smoothing her pretty white dress, and her blue eyes automatically closed. I did wish she had brown eyes like mine, but the blue ones were pretty.

"My baby," I told the other girls, "was very sick. She had a runny nose, and a fever, and goosebumps, and she was turning purple. I took her to the doctor, and she's all better now."

"I took my baby to the doctor too," Verna said. "She had a fever of two hundred and ten. I got her some pink medicine, and she's all better too."

"My daddy is a doctor, and he takes care of my baby," Scarlet said. "She doesn't get sick at all."

"Wow," Verna said, clearly impressed.

"My baby's hungry," I said. My brown braid flopped over my shoulder as I leaned forward to grab my plastic toy baby bottle.

Scarlet's doll got unceremoniously dumped out of her lap as she rose and announced, "I need to pee."

Off she toddled down a hallway, past the kitchen with its gossiping ladies, to the bathroom. Meanwhile, I was feeding my baby. The toy bottle, I thought, was amazing. When I turned it upside-down, it appeared to drain the milk, and when I turned it right-side up, the milk came back. How did it do that? Somewhere in my consciousness I heard the toilet flush, and Scarlet seemed to be taking quite a while to return, but my mind was focused on this magical bottle, tipping it over and righting it again.

A shadow cast on me, and I glanced up to see Scarlet's three feet and five inches towering above. Her eyes narrowed; lips tightened. Her fingers curled into a fist, she drew her arm back, then bashed me right in the nose.

Something crunched, blood spurt. I wailed like a banshee from the pain. What was going on? Why would my friend turn on me like that?

Of course, my caterwauling brought the ladies, including Mommy, rushing into the living room. My fingers tried to hold back the blood dripping down my chin and plopping onto my pink sundress. I knew better than to spill any kind of liquid on carpeting. That was a huge offense at our house, one deserving punishment—at least if I did it, although I had noticed that if any adults spilled something on our carpet, somehow that was always a forgivable accident.

One of the ladies cried, "I'll get some ice!" and dashed out of the room.

I gazed up at my mother. Her curly brown hair flopped forward as she sank to her knees in front of me. "What did you do?"

For crying out loud, why did she always suppose I was responsible? At home, anytime anything went awry, the presumption was that I must have done something to cause it. If a magazine went missing, I must have taken it off the coffee table—even if I'd never touched it. If the drain for the bathroom sink clogged, I must have deliberately done it because I just happened to be the last person to wash my hands there.

I was always assumed guilty until proven innocent. Often I felt like I had to walk on eggshells. And how could I prove I hadn't done something when I didn't know who actually had?

This time, however, I knew who the guilty party was.

I pointed at Scarlet. "She hit me!"

"Scarlet!" Mrs. Hansen demanded. "Did you hit Markette?"

Scarlet gazed up at her mother, eyes wide with fake innocence. "No, Mommy."

"She did too!" I insisted.

Meanwhile, a small bundle of ice in a washcloth arrived, and my mother applied it to my nose. The ladies turned their attention to Verna, who had observed the whole incident.

"Verna?" her mother asked. "Did Scarlet hit Markette?

Verna's blue eyes were already so wide at this unexpected turn of events that her lids barely showed. I glanced at Scarlet. Her eyes were once again narrowed, her lips a thin line, and her hand was clenched in a new fist. It was obvious to me she was silently telling Verna *If you tattle, the same thing will happen to you!*

Were grown-ups idiots? How could they not see Scarlet threatening Verna? But their attention was on the blonde girl and not the red-headed one.

Verna gulped. And caved. "No."

"Then how," my mother asked, "did she get

hurt?"

"Um . . . she fell down."

"That's right!" Scarlet blurted so quickly that I didn't see how anybody could believe her. "She fell down!"

Really? How could I have fallen down? I was sitting on the floor!

But not for long. My mother stood, yanked me to my feet, and smacked my rear. "That," she said, "is for lying!"

You may be shocked at a parent spanking a kid. I understand that in the 21st century, parents are frowned on for spanking. When I was growing up, parents were frowned on if they *didn't* spank their kids.

"You apologize right now!" my mother demanded.

Huh? I was silent, my brain trying to absorb what didn't make sense. Why, all of a sudden, had my sweet little world turned into a painful nightmare? And what did the word *apologize* mean? I'd never heard it before. How could I apologize if I didn't know what it meant to apologize? But grown-ups always thought we kids should already know these things.

My rear got another smack. "Apologize!"

"What?" I cried. "What's 'pologize?" Didn't anybody care that I was in pain? And getting in more pain by the second?

Smack! "Tell her you're sorry!"

"For what?" I blubbered.

Smack! "For lying about her!"

Tears filled my eyes. "I didn't lie!"

Smack! "Of course you did! Why would Scarlet hit you?"

I had no idea. You are also probably wondering what, in such a short period of time, could have motivated my good friend Scarlet to turn on me. Well, Scarlet did have a reason, but I didn't find out what it was until years later, after I died.

It took several more smacks before I capitulated. "I'm sorry!"

I was not sorry.

My mother gathered me up. "I think I should take her home."

Mrs. Hansen scooped up my doll and bottle. "Let me help you."

Mommy glanced at the spot where I had been sitting. "She didn't get any blood on the carpet, did she?" she asked, as though that possibility was the worst thing that could have happened here.

Oh, I got that message. Carpeting: Important. Me: Not so much.

"No, I don't see any stain," Mrs. Hansen said. Apparently it did not occur to anyone that if I'd gotten a bloody nose in a fall, there would be.

"I don't know if I'll ever get it out of her dress," Mommy grumbled. "It's probably ruined." This earned me a glare because of course clothes cost money and ruining something was a capital offense.

I counted myself lucky I wasn't getting spanked for that too.

* * *

I stood on a stepstool and gazed into the bathroom mirror over the sink. My nose was a swollen black and blue mess. Worse, the bottom of it tilted to my right a bit, and it was hard to breathe through it. I touched it for a second and winced in pain.

"That," my father said to my mother, "is definitely broken."

Daddy was still in his dark gray work clothes. Plumbing often meant getting dirty and sweaty. He was already mostly bald, and what strands were left of his brown hair were swept across his scalp in a poor attempt at a comb over.

Mommy said, "The question is: should we make an appointment with the doctor?"

What? A doctor could fix this? Hallelujah!

"And where are we going to get the money for that?" Daddy asked.

I sighed. Oh. Right. Money.

You'd think that by 1959 The Great Depression would be over. According to the history books, it had ended twenty years ago. Well, not at our house. Because Daddy was self-employed, we had no medical insurance.

Mommy said, "Maybe I should write Uncle Mark and ask if he can help."

"Oh no," Daddy said. "We are not going to treat him like a piggybank. You think I want him to believe I can't support my family?"

"Well, obviously you can't. You know, my friend Evelyn has a huge house and a pool—"

"Here we go again!" Daddy grouched.

"If you would just ask him for a job," Mommy pleaded.

"I am not working for somebody else!" he shouted. "I own my own business! I will be my own man!"

"I'll bet you won't turn down any inheritance he leaves you," Mommy said.

Daddy stormed out of the bathroom. "That's different!" he yelled in the hall.

"That nose is your own fault," Mommy remarked, turning back to me. "That's what you get for being clumsy. But don't you worry. I'll write your Great-uncle Mark. We'll get it fixed somehow."

I frowned. What did the word *clumsy* mean? Did it mean lying? I hadn't lied!

But what was the use of saying that? I didn't want to get punished yet again for telling the truth.

Mommy stomped out the door. Moments later, my parents' argument escalated in the living room, their voices rising in volume. I stared at my face a while longer. A couple of tears dribbled down my cheek.

I would have cried much harder if I'd known then what this broken nose would lead to.

Have you ever seen a row of dominoes and how when one falls down, the rest follow suit?

I didn't know it at the time, but this was the first domino tipping over in a sequence of events that would eventually lead to my death.

2

A couple of weeks later, Mommy brought me back to the Hansen's house.

Of course she did. Did I mention that she and Mrs. Hansen were best friends from high school? Yeah, I think I did.

I got only two steps through their front door when Scarlet pointed at me and burst into laughter. "Your nose looks funny!"

It did. The swelling and bruising were gone, but the bottom still veered to the right.

"Scarlet!" her mother scolded. "We do not treat our guests like that! You will apologize immediately!"

By now we both knew what that word meant. "Sorry," Scarlet said in a tone that betrayed she was anything but.

Somehow it was enough to placate her mother. "Now, you girls be nice. Scarlet has a new game she wants to play with you."

Scarlet began, "But I didn't say I wanted—"

A glare from her mother cut her off. Her shoulders slumped. "Okay, let's play."

The moment our mothers' backs were turned, Scarlet yanked my braid.

"Ow!"

"Is something wrong?" Mommy asked.

Scarlet glared at me in an obvious threat.

"No," I said, gazing at the floor.

While our mothers had coffee and chatted in the

living room, Scarlet brought a box of Candy Land to the kitchen table, opened it, and spread out the board. After a quick explanation of the rules, she grabbed a plastic gingerbread man as her playing piece.

"I always play with the red one," she said. "It's a pretty color, like my ponytail. And everybody knows ponytails are better than braids like yours, especially brown ones." She then compared the color of my hair to something which I am too much of a lady to mention.

Soreness ringed my throat. But Scarlet wasn't done.

"No wonder your Daddy's a plumber who works with toilets."

I sat back in my chair. What had I done to prompt this?

Scarlet got involved with the game, and she was consistently far ahead of me on our way to the Candy Castle. After a while, I realized she was cheating. Somehow she would never fall on a square that involved a penalty, even if she should have. She was obviously going to win . . . until I drew the card for the Ice Cream Floats, which advanced me close to the end.

Her jaw dropped. "That's not fair!"

"But that's the rules," I said, scooting my blue piece along the path to the proper square.

She glared at me a moment. A violent flick of her wrist upset the board, cards and game pieces clattering onto the table and floor.

It made enough noise to draw our mothers from

the living room. "What is going on in here?" Mrs. Hansen asked.

Scarlet pointed an accusing finger at me. "She cheats! And she didn't like that I was winning, so she threw everything on the table!"

This time my jaw dropped.

And, apparently, I was not innocent until proven guilty. My mother assumed I was guilty, period.

I was tugged out of my chair and spanked, three swift smacks. Why couldn't she see that Scarlet's statement was contradictory? If I had been cheating, why was Scarlet supposedly winning?

Mommy's hand clamped onto my wrist. She dragged me into the living room so fast that my feet had to race to keep me from stumbling.

She dropped to her knees. "Why can't you play nice?" she whispered into my ear.

"But Mommy, I didn't—"

"I don't want to hear it! We are guests in this house. You will go back, apologize, and let Scarlet win the game."

Well, I knew what would happen if I didn't apologize. At least this time I knew what *apologize* meant.

Having no choice, I shuffled into the kitchen. Gazing at the floor, I mumbled, "I'm sorry."

When I glanced up, Scarlet's smile was smug. The board was cleared and the game started a second time. I knew if I didn't let her win, I'd get spanked again. But how was I supposed to do that? This game was all luck and no skill whatsoever.

Fortunately for me, Scarlet was incredibly good

at cheating.

* * *

From then on, it was pretty much the same thing every time I was thrown together with Scarlet. She'd create a situation, claim innocence, and I'd get blamed and spanked. If Verna was there too, she always backed up whatever Scarlet said. I guess we were both afraid of her, although why she picked on me alone I had no idea.

As you can imagine, I dreaded visits to the Hansens. Having to apologize for being a victim got old fast. I tried pleading illness, fatigue, anything to keep from being dumped into our green '57 Chevy and driven there every time Mommy wanted to visit. All to no avail.

One morning at the breakfast table I was munching my Cheerios and scanning the back of the box. I'd already learned to read quite a bit from the words on various cereal boxes. I was sounding out *milk* when Mommy interrupted me.

"You're starting school next week."

A smile spread across my face. School! Learning! Other kids . . . oh, wait.

I laid down my spoon. "Is Scarlet going too?"

"She's also starting kindergarten, but unfortunately she'll be going to the other school."

That didn't sound unfortunate to me.

Our town, you see, was essentially divided into two. On one side of Main Street were the nice expensive houses, mostly two-story structures with pools. Some, like the ones across the street from the golf course, were even mansions with tennis courts.

We lived on the other side of Main in the poorer section, what you might call the wrong side of the tracks. Here were two-or-three bedroom houses, all one floor and all in the same boring pink stucco.

There were two public elementary schools, and Main Street was not only the demarcation between our town's classes, it was the line our school district had drawn to determine which children attended which school.

Guess which one everyone thought bestowed a better education.

Right. You don't need to guess.

However, my judgment of which was superior was based solely on who would, or wouldn't, be attending with me.

I sighed with relief and returned to making out words on the back of the cereal box. No Scarlet at my school!

* * *

Kindergarten was a blissful heaven on Earth. That's because it's where I met Linda.

Linda had straight brown hair with bangs, like I did, although she got to wear hers free instead of in a braid like Mommy constantly insisted on weaving into my hair.

I guess kids who look alike naturally gravitate toward one another. Maybe it's the familiarity.

But oh how I wished I could have my hair free like Linda's! I loved the way sunlight reflected off it when we designed castles in the playground's sandbox, the way it slipped forward off her shoulders when she leaned over to get another color during fingerpainting. So pretty! And Linda got to wear headbands! They came in all kinds of patterns and colors, which made her even prettier.

One morning in the bathroom while Mommy was brushing my hair, I ventured a hint.

"You know," I said, "it would be a lot less work if you didn't have to braid my hair."

That ought to have done it, right? Less work for you, Mommy!

I knew better than to ask for a headband, which would cost money. But I should also have known better than to contradict one of my mother's ideas.

"You are having a braid," she stated, as usual yanking my hair into a rubber band so tightly it's a wonder I wasn't scalped. It always hurt but I knew complaining wouldn't do any good. I also knew the rubber band would be painfully yanked out at bedtime, along with a few hairs. That was to save it for the next day, even though we got two new rubber bands every day that came with the morning and afternoon newspapers.

That's because Mommy fastened the rubber band so tightly into my hair that sometimes it broke.

Did I mention The Depression wasn't over at our house? Nothing was wasted, ever.

"How about a ponytail?" I asked. "Scarlet wears ponytails." And, according to her, everybody knew ponytails were better.

"You," Mommy said, dividing my hair into three sections, "are not Scarlet."

I sighed. The braid was getting longer every day. Already it dropped below my shoulder blades.

Oh, well. At least I was going to get to spend the day with Linda!

* * *

All too soon fingerpainting and story times were gone, and I was back in summer vacation with the obligatory visits to Scarlet's house.

But summer did have one bright spot, and that showed up on a Saturday when Daddy was watching baseball on TV.

Daddy always sat in a fake leather brown recliner, and nobody dared interrupt him when he was watching sports. He would stay glued to that chair unless a commercial was being broadcast or the game was over. He was so obsessed with sports he'd ask Mommy to serve Thanksgiving dinner only at halftime during a football game, as if, when she slid the turkey into the oven hours earlier, she could judge exactly when that was going to be. If dinner was done before then, my parents let it get cold and let me starve while the teams called one delaying timeout after another.

You see, back than you couldn't pause a television show. Nobody even had a remote control. Programs had to be watched when they were on, and in black and white. The TV antenna on our roof picked up seven channels from Los Angeles, and, unlike most people back then, we were lucky to get so many.

Oh, and I had to be absolutely quiet and never, ever come between Daddy and the TV, blocking his view of the set. It was another offense meriting a spanking.

On this particular day the doorbell rang. Daddy yelled, "Somebody get that!"

"I'm busy in the kitchen!" Mommy called. It seemed like Mommy was always busy in the kitchen.

Ding dong!

"Markette!" Daddy ordered. "Get the door!"

You may very well wonder about the wisdom of allowing a six-year-old girl to answer a door when it was unknown who was on the other side. But that's the way things were back in 1960.

Since I was on the far side of the room, I had to crawl through the space in front of the TV to avoid blocking Daddy's view. I opened the door to find a man of about sixty years wearing horn-rimmed glasses. His bushy brown hair was graying at the temples,

"Great-uncle Mark!" I squealed, bobbing up and down on my toes in excitement. "Mommy! Daddy! It's Great-uncle Mark!"

He stepped into the living room and scooped me off my feet. I hugged his neck.

To my utter shock, Daddy rose from his chair and turned the TV off. Wow. He *never* did that! Not during sports!

Only years later did I realize he would of course give his full attention to the man he expected to someday inherit millions from.

The picture on the TV screen shrank into a white dot that slowly faded as Great-uncle Mark set me down. I knew exactly what was coming next. Whenever he visited, he always leaned over, tapped the tip of my nose, and asked, "How's my little princess?"

As I expected, he began his usual routine. "And how's my little—" His finger froze and his eyes widened. Straightening up, he said, "Harold! I thought I sent you money for the surgery to get this girl's nose fixed."

"Oh," Daddy said. "Um . . . we had some unexpected expenses."

We did? I wondered as Mommy stepped out of the kitchen, drying her hands on a dish towel.

Great-uncle Mark's lips tightened and his nose scrunched up a bit. I was still wondering about those unexpected expenses. Maybe they had something to do with the new refrigerator my parents had gotten when ours broke.

"And work has been very slow lately," Daddy added, frowning.

"How long are you staying?" I blurted. "Are you staying forever?" I could only hope. Please, please, please!

Daddy's face softened at the change of subject.

"Oh, not quite that long," Great-uncle Mark said. "I had some business in Los Angeles that wrapped up early, so I thought I would stop by."

Mommy said, "This is quite a surprise. I hope you will stay for dinner."

He held up a hand. "I don't want to put you out."

"Oh, there's plenty, as long as you like roast beef."

Great-uncle Mark grinned. "I never turn down a home-cooked meal. And . . . I also might have something in one of my pockets, just in case there happens to be a princess in this house."

Honestly, his being there was more than gift enough, but I wasn't about to turn down a present. My bobbing up and down started again while he made a pretense of patting each of his pockets in a search.

"Ah! Here it is!" he said, yanking a little flat box out of his jacket.

With great flourish, he handed it to me. "Your Highness!"

I could not get that box open fast enough. Within glittered a golden necklace with a cross.

"Oh! It's so beautiful! Thank you!"

"Well," he said, turning me around, "let's see if it fits and is fit for a princess."

Wringing my hands, I nervously waited while he fastened the chain around my neck. Oh, my goodness. What if it didn't fit? What if he declared I was too small for it? I was already having to wait to grow into a few of the clothes Mommy had gotten for me at our local thrift store.

I turned back around. "Is it okay?" *Please, please, please let it be okay! Please let it be the right size!*

He nodded. "You look beautiful. It's definitely fit for a princess."

"I'm never going to take it off, never!"

Great-uncle Mark laughed. "Don't you think you should if you're going to take a bath?"

"Okay, then. But no other time!"

"What if you go swimming?"

"Okay, then too, but no other time!"

"What about when you're sleeping? You wouldn't want to break the chain in your sleep."

Was there no end to these restrictions? "Okay, then too, but no other time! I'll wear it the rest of my life!"

Just so you know, I kept true to my word.

That's right. I was wearing it when I died.

3

We had some time before dinner, so Great-uncle Mark dropped onto his hands and knees. "Who wants a horsey ride?"

I squealed, "I do!" and flung one leg over his back.

Later in life I often wondered what my great-uncle's clients and employees would have thought of this powerful entrepreneur down on the living room rug with a six-year-old girl riding his back. Great-uncle Mark snorted, whinnied, pawed the air with his "hooves." I giggled as we scampered around the coffee table twice, then down the hall.

"Hurry up, horsey!"

That produced more excited whinnying and a raising of his "forelegs" so far I had to grab onto his neck for dear life. The Lone Ranger would have been proud of his horse Silver rearing so high. I lost my grip and slid off, both of us screeching with laughter.

I gazed through the doorway to my bedroom and jumped to my feet. "I have something to show you!"

"What is it?" Great-uncle Mark asked, rising.

I grabbed a book off my bed and proudly displayed it before him. "I checked this out of the library!"

"*The Blue Book of Fairy Tales*," he read. "You have a library card? You checked it out yourself?"

Mommy stepped into the hall. "She's had a

library card since she was three," she said proudly.

"Since she was *three*?"

"All I had to do to get it was print my name," I said, "on the card inside the book." I flipped open the cover. "I can read it too. Would you like to hear a story?"

"Oh, I don't think Uncle Mark would want to do that," Mommy said.

"Oh, yes I would!" Great-uncle Mark said, scooping me off my feet and carrying me, book and all, into the living room. We plopped onto the sofa, and I began "Once upon a time . . ."

* * *

Before bedtime I had my bath. I wanted to slip on my golden cross afterward, but I remembered I wasn't supposed to wear it to bed. Just so you know, I did keep my promise as much as possible, looping it around my neck every morning.

Mommy left me alone to get into my green pajamas, which I donned as fast as I could. I didn't want to miss a single moment with Great-uncle Mark, so I scooted out of the bathroom once I was done.

I came to a screeching halt in the hall as I realized he and my parents were sitting at the kitchen table, talking about me.

"She's awfully smart," Great-uncle Mark was saying. "A library card at three. At six she's reading well above her age level."

"She must take after you," Daddy said, never missing an opportunity to compliment the man he hoped would be his someday benefactor.

"Where will she be going to school for first grade?"

"The same place she attended kindergarten," Mommy said.

"A public school?"

"Why not?" Daddy said. "We pay taxes for that, don't we?"

Great-uncle Mark had a firmness in his voice I had never heard before. "No. That girl should get the best private education money can buy. And I am going to see to it."

"Surely you're not talking about boarding school?" Mommy pleaded. "You wouldn't think of sending her away from us, would you?"

Send me away from Mommy and Daddy? Oh, no! Well, maybe that would be okay if I got to live with Great-uncle Mark instead.

"I am a bit tempted," he said. "I can see how well you've taken care of her nose. And I assume you will repay yourselves the money you used for your unexpected expenses and take care of it. But, getting back to her schooling, what other options are here in town?"

"Well, there's St. Andrew's," Daddy offered. "For grades one through eight."

"A Catholic school?"

"Yes," Daddy replied.

"You mean to tell me," Great-uncle Mark said, "that there's a school in your parish, and you weren't even considering sending her there? Her religious upbringing is far more important than her intellectual one."

I frowned. What did the word *intellectual* mean?

"The tuition—" Daddy began.

"—will be paid by me," Great-uncle Mark interrupted. "Along with her book bill plus any other expenses, such as her uniform."

I bit my lip. I wasn't going to return to the same school? What about being with my friend Linda?

"That would be wonderful!" Mommy gushed. "Her best friend, Scarlet, will be going there too!"

My eyes widened in dismay. Oh no! No, no, no! I'd be going to the same school as Scarlet?

No Linda? Scarlet instead?

Could I talk them out of this? I realized Great-uncle Mark was only trying to help. If I said anything, wouldn't I disappoint him? He thought he was giving me something wonderful. And it cost money! I already knew from my parents how precious money was.

"Thank you," Daddy said. "If you send us a check every month, we will take care of it."

"The way you took care of her nose? What if some new unexpected expenses arise? No. I will have my secretary make arrangements directly with the school. Speaking of Markette, where is she, anyway?"

At that I made my appearance in the kitchen, but I couldn't hide my distress. My lower lip trembled and tears budded in my eyes.

"Princess?" Great-uncle Mark asked, gathering me onto his lap. "What's wrong?"

I hugged his neck, my pajamaed front heaving with sobs against his chest. Over his shoulder I told him only one of the two reasons I was upset. "You won't be here when I wake up."

"Oh, princess," he said. "I'm sorry I have to leave. But my business takes me all over the world. I'll be back, I promise."

My arms tightened around his neck. I cried like my heart was breaking.

Because it was.

* * *

We had a floor-length mirror on the inside of the bathroom door, and I gazed at my reflection in it. Stiffly ironed white shirt with Peter Pan collar, blue plaid jumper, bobby socks and oxford shoes.

Brown hair in bangs along with the obligatory tight braid fastened with a newspaper rubber band.

Oh, also the necklace Great-uncle Mark had gifted me. We weren't allowed to wear jewelry at school unless it was religious. My golden cross qualified.

In the kitchen Mommy handed me my Minnie Mouse lunchbox. I knew it contained half of a peanut butter sandwich, an apple, and an oatmeal cookie. The school provided pints of cold milk to those students whose parents had paid for them, and Great-uncle Mark had generously opted for an entire year's worth.

At the front door Mommy kissed my forehead. "Bye, bye, God bless, and be good. Look both ways before crossing the street, and don't step in any ink."

Okay, you're probably wondering why she mentioned not stepping in ink. It's because this is what her mother had always said to her when she'd started out for school. Back when my mother was young, schools had inkwells, and if spillage occurred, shoes could get ruined. I took her admonishment as a reminder not to get my uniform dirty.

I set off down our suburban street toward school. It was a bright sunny day, birds chirping in some jacaranda trees, but I wasn't thrilled. No Linda today. And what might Scarlet do to me?

You may also wonder about a six-year-old girl walking to school by herself instead of being driven. But gas was a whopping 32.9¢! That may not sound like much, but a candy bar cost a nickel. An ice cream cone cost a nickel. So it was essentially spending the same for six and a half of those for only one gallon of gas. Besides, I had already walked by myself to kindergarten, and everybody thought it was safe.

Back then all children walked to school . . . and everywhere else, for that matter, if the weather allowed it and the place they were going was close enough.

Unfortunately.

I was standing at the corner of Main and Elm, waiting for the light to turn green, when my braid was yanked, hard, from behind.

"Hey, it's Crook Nose!"

I winced, partly from the pain and partly from recognizing whose voice that was.

Scarlet.

I turned around. Yup, Scarlet and a couple of other girls were dressed in the same uniform. Verna was one, along with another girl with short blonde hair. I later learned her name was Damara.

"Wow," Damara said. "That is the ugliest nose I've ever seen."

Great. Scarlet had not one minion but two. Three against one. I did not like those odds.

Scarlet of course had to improve on what Damara had said. She would not let such an opportunity pass by. "Probably the ugliest nose in the world."

The girls laughed hysterically. Scarlet shoulder-shoved me aside as the light changed. Since it was so unexpected, I lost my balance and almost fell. My "clumsiness" provoked another burst of laughter. Their snickering continued as they crossed the street. Having no choice, I followed behind.

We had three more blocks to go. Scarlet and her followers used the time to occasionally glance back at me, whisper to each other—obviously about me—then giggle again, sometimes so loudly they snorted. I had no idea what they were saying, but it couldn't be good.

Of course that was part of their intended torture, to make me anxious about whatever they were telling one another.

I sighed. First grade was going to be awful.

Inside the classroom, our teacher, Sister Rose, was as big as a whale and dressed in a black habit with a black veil, although a span of white arched over her forehead at the front of the veil like a headband. I was a bit intimidated by her size until I saw she had a beautiful smile. When she stepped aside, I got the surprise of my life.

Linda! Linda was on the other side of the room!

We both squealed, rushed to each other, and hugged, bouncing up and down on our toes.

I glanced at Scarlet. Her mouth was turned down at this unexpected turn of events. I had a friend.

And she didn't like that. Not one little bit.

She especially didn't like it later during recess when Linda and I were standing in line for the slide and she tried to tug my braid again. Linda, fire blazing in her eyes, stomped her foot and stepped between us. "Markette is my friend!" she declared. "You leave her alone!"

Bless you, Linda!

I had more than a friend.

I had a champion.

4

Unfortunately for me, although Linda lived on the same side of Main Street as I did, she was north of Elm Avenue, while I was south. This meant she walked a different route to school, which left me at the mercy of Scarlet, et al, during trips coming and going.

Not that they had any mercy.

As the weeks passed, I tried to avoid them by leaving home early or running part of the way so I could beat them to school. I also started leaving late for home, hoping they'd already be far ahead of me. The first one worked pretty well, not so much the second.

For one thing, I couldn't wait too long to leave school or Mommy would worry. And boy, did I hear about it if I were late! That, apparently, was a spankable offense. I invented all kinds of reasons she wouldn't object to in order to stick around the classroom, like cleaning the board for Sister Rose and clapping chalk dust out of erasers. I bet Sister Rose never realized why I was so eager to help.

But Scarlet and company sometimes waited for me at the intersection of Main and Elm so they could get their daily dose of "Tormenting Markette." I wanted to detour onto side streets, but I had to cross Elm, and it had a speed limit of 35. The one time I did try, cars whizzed by frighteningly fast even though they should have stopped because I had stepped into the crosswalk. I gave up and headed back to Main and Elm. It was the only signalized intersection I could use.

I endured a lot of braid pulling and shoving. Most of the torture was insults like "Crook Nose," "stupid," and their favorite, "ugly."

Boys bully with their fists. Girls, for the most part, bully with their tongues.

I'd been told "Sticks and stones may break my bones, but names will never harm me."

Yeah. Right. Whoever had made that up obviously wasn't talking about emotional harm.

One sunny afternoon while we were on our way home from second grade, Scarlet gave me her greatest insult so far. "Why don't you do the world a favor?" she snickered over her shoulder as she and her buddies stepped back onto the curb after crossing at the intersection of Main and Elm. "Why don't you just drop dead?"

This of course was followed by peals of laughter.

When I finished crossing the street a few steps behind them, I stood on the corner for a moment, tears streaming down my face. Then I took off for home, running so hard my lungs ached and I was out of breath. That was the last straw! I'd had it!

I was going to risk telling Mommy. Maybe I'd get spanked for lying. But I had to do *something*!

When I got home, I plopped down on the sofa, and, as my mother stood before me, I told her all about the insults. I didn't tell her about the shoving and braid-pulling—I knew she'd never believe that. No, not from her best friend's daughter.

I wound the whole thing up with "And she told me to drop dead!"

Gazing up at my mother's face, I hoped she would tell me what to do about it. I hoped that, if I couldn't get any advice, at the very least I'd get some sympathy. I even imagined Mommy hugging me and telling me she would take care of it.

I sure didn't expect what I did get.

Laughter.

"Markette," she giggled, shaking her head, "all kids say things like that sometimes. It doesn't mean anything. My goodness, you are far too sensitive."

Oh, I got the implication of that. My pain, she was telling me, was *my* fault. What, did she think I was deliberately choosing to hurt?

I tried again as fresh tears formed along my lower lids. "You don't understand. She did mean it!"

Please! I was thinking. *Can't you tell how much I'm hurting? You are a mother whose child is in pain! Help me!*

Instead, Mommy started reciting a little poem that started "Nobody likes me." The poem had to do with worms. I'm not going to tell it to you because I don't want to violate any copyright laws, and I also don't want to give you the same horrible nausea that began building in my stomach from listening to it in my mother's mocking tone. If you really want to read it, I suppose you can look it up on the internet people have nowadays, but you shouldn't if you've just eaten.

Remember, you were warned!

I'd had lunch hours before, but that didn't help. I

was already emotionally upset, and the poem only made me more nauseated.

What was left in my stomach vaulted up in one gigantic heave.

Did I mention that our living room was carpeted?

Did I mention that my mother was standing right in front of me?

Wearing shoes?

Wearing *brand new* shoes?

I'd never been spanked so hard in my life.

I resolved that I would never ask an adult for help with my bullies ever again.

Ever.

* * *

For the most part, I loved school, at least what we did inside the classroom. I was absolutely amazed that one of the subjects was reading. To me, reading was recreation, not study! It wasn't boring like memorizing addition and subtraction tables. We actually got a subject that was more than fun.

One bad thing about school, though, besides the bullying, was grades. I began to think grades were invented so parents had an excuse to berate their children.

Not that my parents ever needed much of an excuse.

My grades weren't awful, mind you. It's just that I got criticized for the tiniest thing.

For example, one time I brought home a spelling test of twenty words. I had misspelled one. You'd think it was the end of the world the way

Mommy carried on. "How on earth did you miss that one? Didn't you study?" Sheesh! She didn't say anything about the nineteen I got right. It was as if those other words didn't even exist.

The next week, when I got all twenty right, I proudly showed her my test. This time I'd get some praise, right?

Wrong! What I got was "If you're so smart, how come you missed that word last week?"

Worst of all was my report card. How I dreaded bringing that home twice a year. This I was required to show to Daddy, the biggest critic on planet Earth. It was never, ever, ever, ever, ever, ever, ever—okay, you get the idea—good enough.

Ever.

Sorry, I just had to put one more "ever" in there.

Halfway through second grade, there I stood in the living room, sweating bullets, waiting for a commercial to come on TV so I could show it to him without interrupting his show.

Finally, a break in the broadcast. It was an animated ad with characters from *The Flintstones* touting Winston cigarettes, and it showed both Fred and Barney smoking.

No, I am not kidding. There really used to be cigarette commercials on TV, and there really was a cartoon ad that promoted smoking aimed at children. You can look it up on the internet if you don't believe me.

Without a word, I handed the report card to him. He glanced at it, then up at me with The Look.

If you've ever been a child—and of course you

have—you know exactly what it means to get The Look from a parent.

My shoulders slumped.

It's true I had a couple of B's, but . . .

"This grade in science," Daddy said. "A B-? Why wasn't that at least a B? And this B+ in math. Why wasn't that an A-?"

He said nothing about the rest of the grades, which were all A's.

Signing it, he added, "I expect better next time. Your Great-uncle Mark is paying a lot of money for you to go to that school. I'd hate for him to be disappointed in you."

Remember when I told you about dominos toppling over in a sequence that would lead to my death?

It may surprise you, but this was one of those dominos.

5

I thought I should tell you, just so you know a little bit about what's coming up, that we haven't gotten to the most important character in the story yet. Yes, I know: here we are in chapter 5, and I haven't even mentioned this person.

I will get to him later. Or maybe I should say he got to me later.

Third grade was the year I really began to discover the disparity between different classes of people. After all, Scarlet was very happy to point out to me every instance in which she was superior, like how much bigger her house was, and how she got to wear pretty bows in her hair when all I got was a rubber band.

To my amazement, even the Tooth Fairy seemed to know which kids were more valuable. I couldn't figure out why a fairy would want my discarded baby teeth, but I wasn't about to turn down free cash. I received a dime under my pillow while Scarlet not only got a dollar, it was a silver dollar coin. Why was the Tooth Fairy so much nicer to her? How come her teeth were worth ten times as much? And if they were, how could the Tooth Fairy tell the difference?

Luckily for me, good old Santa didn't seem to discriminate against me, although I was certain my abundance of gifts had something to do with Great-uncle Mark. He'd call a few weeks before Christmas, ask what I wanted, and claim he would pass on the information to Santa himself because he had Santa's phone number. And I believed him!

Well, what else was I supposed to believe? Everything on my list ended up under the Christmas tree each year, so it had to be true, right?

Well, almost everything. The one gift I repeatedly requested but which Santa couldn't slip under the tree was a visit from Great-uncle Mark, even though I told him I wanted that more than all the other presents combined. Great-uncle Mark always choked up a bit on the phone when I asked for that and promised to try to deliver it himself but was never able to.

Another thing I didn't understand about Christmas was that while I would have put Scarlet in the Naughty category rather than the Nice one, she always bragged about the many expensive presents she reaped in each yuletide season. I thought Santa could see us when we were sleeping, knew when we were awake, so wasn't he watching when Scarlet bullied me? How could he know if we'd been bad or good and not know about any of what she was doing to me?

One Saturday I was in my bedroom, reading *The Lion, the Witch, and the Wardrobe* and listening to the transistor radio Great-uncle Mark had told Santa about last Christmas. The Shirelles were warbling "Will You Still Love Me Tomorrow," and I was humming along with the tune.

Mom entered with a brand new hot pink ceramic piggybank that I figured she must have found at a thrift store. It was kind of a gaudy, ugly thing with bright blue flowers painted on it, and it had a slot in the top of the piggy's back. It also said "For My Cadillac" along the side, as though someone would use this to save up for a car, especially a luxury car.

That's why I assumed it had been purchased at a thrift store, even though it was new. It was where Mom usually shopped, and who would pay full price for something so tacky?

"We are going to start giving you an allowance," Mom proclaimed.

Excitement built inside me. I knew from Scarlet pointing it out that she got a dollar bill a week. A whole dollar! Twenty candy bars' worth! Or twenty ice cream cones! Or ten candy bars and ten ice cream cones, or . . . well, you get the idea.

The only time I ever got any money was if I chanced upon some coins lying by the side of the road or lost a tooth. Or if I returned a soda bottle I'd found on my way home from school.

Back then, before the recycling programs you have today, soda bottles were returned to bottling plants to be refilled. If I found one and turned it in at a store, I was rewarded with three cents. Two soda bottles were enough to buy a candy bar with a penny to spare.

Mom proudly handed me a quarter. "Here! Put it into your piggy!"

I tried to keep my shoulders from slumping. No dollar? Only a quarter? Oh, well, better than nothing, right?

I took the coin and dropped it through the slot. Shaking the pig a bit, I heard it rattling inside.

Then I checked the bottom of the pig. Unlike most piggybanks, this one did not have a rubber stopper that could be pulled out to release the money. Another reason why it was probably at a thrift store.

"How do you get it back out?" I asked.

"When it's full, we'll get a hammer and break the pig!"

Wait a minute. What?

"You'll get another quarter to put in next week," Mom said. "Won't that be nice?"

Yeah. Great. Really nice. From the size of this bank, it would take me years to fill it.

My money was not my money to spend? This was an allowance I wasn't allowed?

"Thank you, Mom," I said listlessly. I thanked her only because she was expecting it. Honestly, I was tempted to say "Thanks for nothing."

I sighed as she left the room. Guess if I wanted any spending money, I was stuck with returning soda bottles. That, and any coinage the Tooth Fairy might bring.

* * *

One warm May evening Mom announced we were going to the drive-in. *Lilies of the Field* with Sidney Poitier was playing, and my parents wanted to see it.

My shoulders drooped. This was not exactly thrilling news, at least not for me. I would not get to see the film. Oh, I was going along, all right, but as usual I would go in the backseat in my pajamas, with a blanket and a pillow.

The reason for this was because the theatre charged by the vehicle, regardless of the number of people in it. Parents, including mine, saw this as a terrific opportunity to attend the movies without having to pay either for a child's ticket or a sitter.

Mom and Dad were going to get to see a movie. I was going to get to go to sleep in the backseat.

Yay.

The only good thing about this was that I got to go with my hair free instead of in its perpetual braid. Hard to sleep with a braid in my hair. Also, I'd get to watch the cartoon, if there was one.

My mother started popping corn in a pot on the stove. That was another benefit to drive-ins: you could bring your own snacks. As the kernels exploded, the scent was enticing, but I would not be allowed to eat any of it. That's because, as always, I would have to brush my teeth before we left.

"I got you some new pajamas," she said, shaking the bottom of the pot back and forth over the stove's flame. If it were left alone on the burner, the popcorn would scorch. "I laid them out on your bed. Go put them on."

Obediently, I slunk to my room. One look at my new PJs and my heart sank. Oh, no. If there were a prize for the ugliest pajamas ever made, these would win hands down.

They had pictures of cow heads on them, really ugly brown cows with big fat pink tongues lolling out. As I picked them up, I noticed the fabric was stiff with newness. Of course. Once again I was getting something new nobody else wanted that

Mom had found cheap at a thrift store.

Whatever mental picture you're getting of these, trust me, they were more hideous than anything you're envisioning.

I gazed upward. *Why, God? Why me?*

I slipped them on, consoled by the fact that nobody but my parents would see me. It would be almost dark when we arrived at the drive-in, and I could hide in the backseat.

Now of course you don't expect I was actually that lucky.

Because, of course, I wouldn't be mentioning this whole business about the drive-in if I'd actually been that lucky.

Guess whose car parked right next to ours when we pulled into our space at the drive-in. C'mon, guess!

Right. You don't have to guess.

"Markette!" Mom gushed. "Look! Your friend Scarlet's here!"

Please, God, let me die right now.

Scarlet slipped out of the Hansen's car. She was dressed in jeans and a red T-shirt. She was wearing tennis shoes instead of floppy slippers like the pink ones I had on.

Our mothers were also out of the cars almost instantly, gabbing away, thrilled at this wonderful coincidence of running into each other. I slunk down in the backseat, but I couldn't hide completely. Scarlet took one glimpse of me through our car window and snorted with laughter.

Could things possibly get any worse?

Of course they could. But you already knew that, didn't you?

You see, another thing drive-ins usually had was a playground with swings and slides in an area right below the screen, an obvious incentive for parents to bring their children with them and therefore attend.

So our mothers suggested that, until it was time for the movie to start, we go play there.

Together.

With me in my pajamas.

My ugly pajamas.

My ugly cow pajamas.

I immediately objected. "I don't want to play."

"Markette!"

I crossed my fingers behind my back. "I'm tired!"

Mom scooted into the car and whispered in my ear, "You will go play with Scarlet. She shouldn't have to play alone when she has a friend here."

I sighed. I was sure Scarlet would never refer to me as a friend. But obviously there was no getting out of this.

"Fine." I opened the car door.

Scarlet and I started for the playground. Once we were out of our parents' earshot, she sneered, "Those are the ugliest pajamas I've ever seen. But that's what the ugliest girl in the world should wear."

Yeah. Thanks, Mom.

When we got to the swings and slides, Scarlet said, "I don't want to be seen with you. You might get some ugly on me." She slipped onto a swing and started pumping.

I sat on a bench, pulled my legs up and hugged them tightly with my arms, trying to make myself as small as possible. Hot embarrassment flooded my cheeks. I was the only child there in pajamas. In public. With other kids all around.

I'm not going to draw this out by telling you the nasty comments I got from some of the other kids. We were there maybe ten minutes before it was time to return.

It seemed more like ten years.

6

Scarlet got in the front seat of her car and sat between her parents. The Hansen's vehicle, like many at the time, had coach seats so three could sit in the front, and rare was the car that even had seatbelts. I climbed into our back. At least I was out of public view. Dad pulled the drive-in speaker inside, draped its hook onto the rim of the driver's side window glass, then rolled up the window far enough to hold it in place. It played tinny music as a cartoon began.

It was in color, unlike the cartoons broadcast on our black and white TV at home. This, at least, I was always allowed to watch.

Or I should say I was allowed to watch part of the picture. The rear-view mirror blocked about a third of the screen. How could anybody see anything with a mirror in the way?

What I could tell of the cartoon was that it was entitled *Bad Luck Blackie*, and it was about a dog bullying a poor little kitten. Boy, could I sympathize. I wasn't enjoying it much but perked up when a black cat took pity on the kitten and started giving the dog all kinds of bad luck, like a piano plummeting out of the sky right onto him. The cat even gave the kitten a whistle to call him whenever the dog threatened him.

If you want to see it yourself, you can watch at least part of it on your internet.

I loved it, what I could actually view of it. If

only I had a whistle like that. I envisioned a cartoon in which stuff slammed down onto Scarlet each time she tormented me. She'd say something nasty, and *wham*! A steamroller! *Wham*! A battleship!

That'd get her to leave me alone.

All too soon it ended, and Mom said, "Go to sleep."

"Can't I watch the movie?"

"No. You need your sleep."

"But it's about nuns! Scarlet's parents are letting her watch it."

"You're not Scarlet. Besides, you told me you were tired."

Rats. I had told her that when she'd wanted me to go play.

I grabbed my pillow, laid down, and tossed my blanket over me.

I don't know if you've ever tried to sleep in the backseat of a car, but it's not the most comfortable bed in the world. I also had to contend with listening to my parents munching popcorn and the tinny soundtrack of the movie in which, every once in a while, folks started singing a song entitled "Amen."

I stared at the ceiling. *I'm not in a car*, I told myself, squeezing my eyes shut. *I'm a princess riding in a carriage.* I imagined myself wearing a sparkling white gown and golden slippers. My hair was free instead of in a stupid braid. The carriage was an open-air one. Cantering horses, their hooves clopping, drew it down a beautiful country highway full of trees and sweetly fragrant flowers. I added in some townspeople who cheered and waved as I passed by on my way to a castle.

"All hail the princess!" they cried.

Just for good measure, I put Scarlet into my fantasy too. She was standing alongside the road, but she wasn't in a lovely gown like mine. She was of course wearing cow pajamas.

She called me ugly, and right as she scooped up a handful of mud to fling at me, I blew a whistle and a steel-gray aircraft carrier smashed down on her. *Wham!*

That evoked a smile in the backseat.

When I arrived at the castle, I was greeted by the king, who looked an awful lot like Great-uncle Mark. He was dressed in an ermine robe and had a golden crown atop his head. I suddenly realized I hadn't given myself a tiara, so I quickly added one that matched my golden slippers.

The king hugged me and escorted me to a room full of presents and toys packed to the ceiling. Oh! And there was a beautiful white pony, nickering, waiting just for me. I fed her a peanut butter sandwich which she appreciatively gobbled up. Well, peanut butter sandwiches were my favorite, so I figured she would like them too, although they're probably very bad for horses.

This was the pony I had wished for on my last birthday when I'd blown out the candles. I'd been told if I said the wish out loud, it wouldn't come true.

I had remained silent, but somehow the wish hadn't come true anyway.

I was petting the pony's head when the nuns in the movie started singing "Amen" again, tugging me out of my daydream.

Gritting my teeth, I flopped onto my right side, facing the rear of the seat. *It isn't fair*, I told myself. *Why do I have to have parents like them? Why can't I have parents like Scarlet's? She gets to watch the movie. It wouldn't cost any more money to let me watch it. Why do I have to wear ugly pajamas and go to sleep when everybody else gets to have fun?*

I rolled onto my back again and reached for the golden cross Great-uncle Mark had given me, but of course it wasn't there. Couldn't wear it when I was supposed to be sleeping.

God, I prayed. *You can do anything. Please, can't I have some other parents, like Scarlet's? I mean, I don't want mine to die or anything. Just maybe I could be adopted by somebody else? Or please let me go live with Great-uncle Mark. I'll be really good, I promise! I won't ever sin or tell lies, ever. Just let me have that, okay?*

Silence.

Sometimes, I concluded, God was annoyingly silent.

Tears crowded my eyes and slid down the sides of my face.

It was the way life was, and there wasn't anything I could do about it.

* * *

Later, when the movie was over, I was still awake.

As we drove home, amid the rumbling of our

'57 Chevy, I watched the scenery pass by, at least what I could see of it from my perch lying down in the backseat. That late at night, when there was barely any traffic, all the signals were flashing red, turning the intersections into boulevard stops.

We drove right past the spot where, years later, I would die. I was only nine, but already my life was well over half gone.

When we arrived at our house, Mom was furious at me because I hadn't fallen asleep, like she'd instructed me to.

Like I could just do that because she'd commanded it.

I sighed. It seemed I was always in trouble, no matter what.

* * *

"Moo!"

Yeah, I should have known that come Monday the news of my cow pajamas would be all over school. At recess, the moment I was by myself, about to climb onto the jungle gym, Scarlet and her minions, Verna and Damara, surrounded me.

"Moo!" Scarlet said again. "Markette wants to be a cow!"

"A moo cow!" Verna said.

"A moo cow mooing all the time!" Damara added.

"No wonder her name is Markette," Scarlet scoffed, deliberately mispronouncing it to sound like the word *market*. "That's where cows end up, in a meat market."

Oh, if only I really had one of those cartoon

whistles!

But then I had something better. Linda jumped off her swing and dashed over.

"You're the ones doing the mooing," she pointed out. "Sounds like you're the ones who want to be cows."

That shut them up.

Bless you, Linda.

Why couldn't I ever think of a witty retort like that?

7

Come fourth grade we girls were no longer allowed in the play area that had the swings and slides.

Nope, we were banished into the girls' yard. All girls grades 4 through 8 had to share one yard. The boys had to share their yards only with one other grade instead of being lumped together with four other grades. That, I was told, was because they were boys. Great-uncle Mark was paying the same tuition for me as for any boy in the school, but we girls were certainly getting less for the money. Amazingly, I was one of the few who was upset by this. Such discrimination against girls was all too common at the time.

We were not allowed to slip so much as a toe over the line into one of the boys' yards, but the boys were allowed into our yard because that's where the drinking fountain was. This fountain had three faucets, but nobody would so much as sip out of the middle one.

As the sun beat down on me one hot September afternoon, I was standing in line for one of the other spigots. Amid the screeching of five grades of girls at play in one yard, I asked Linda, who was in line behind me, why the middle faucet was off limits.

Linda knew everything. "I heard somebody threw up on it," she stated matter-of-factly. "And ever since it's had poison coming out of it."

Right. The school was supplying poison in one

of its water fountains.

Yet . . . stupid as this was, I kept my position in line. Who knew what kind of teasing I'd get if I dared to defy schoolground lore?

After our drinks, we headed for our classmates. This yard had a basketball court and a volleyball court, but fourth-grade girls were not allowed to use them. We were assigned one four-square with one partly deflated ball. That was it for all fifteen of us.

The four-square had already been taken over by Scarlet, Verna, Damara, and one other girl. I sighed. No play time for me.

Not for a full school year.

At least I had Linda, and Scarlet was preoccupied with winning, cheating if necessary to accomplish that.

* * *

One Friday morning in late November I was at my school desk, trying to figure out a word problem in math. Did I care how much Farmer Brown had to pay for a bale of hay? I was pretty sure I didn't.

Okay, I was absolutely sure I didn't.

Who made up this stuff, anyway? How I hated word problems! But if I didn't do well, it would be reflected on my report card, and I knew what Dad would say about that.

Despite a few smeary erasures, I'd about got the math worked out when one of the eighth-grade girls slipped into the classroom and whispered into Sister Thomas' ear. Sister Thomas was short, old and wrinkled, but kind. I frowned. Whatever the girl had said had caused her to blanch white as a ghost, almost as white as the headband on her black habit. What was going on?

Sister had a little desk bell, and, as soon as the older girl left, her palm dinged it several times. "Boys and girls, please put your pencils down."

Our lesson was being interrupted? This was serious. Little did I know how serious it was.

I was about to find out.

"We've just received word," she said, "that President Kennedy has been shot."

I gasped. What?

"We will pray that he will be all right," she added.

We immediately dropped to our knees next to our desks and bowed our heads in prayer. I started choking and sobbing. Things like that did not happen! Well, I mean, I knew they happened but only a long time ago like with President Lincoln. Not nowadays! Not to someone I knew about! Not to a person I'd seen on TV! Not to someone Great-uncle Mark had actually met in person!

Why would someone deliberately shoot someone else?

Lunch that day was somber. My peanut butter sandwich was tasteless.

We kids could talk about little else. Even the four-square was left vacant, and the yard was far quieter than usual. My nine-year-old brain searched for answers but came up empty. I felt so sorry for President Kennedy's wife. Only a few months before, her baby boy had died when he was only two days old. Now she might lose her husband too.

We didn't know President Kennedy was already dead. It hadn't been announced on the news before we'd gone out to lunch. When we returned to the classroom, Sister told us, and we once again dropped to our knees to pray for the repose of his soul.

That afternoon I plodded home from school, staring at the sidewalk most of the way. Even Scarlet left me alone, for once. I scooped up our afternoon paper off the lawn, carried it inside, and opened it. KENNEDY DEAD the headline proclaimed in large black letters.

He had gotten up that morning and had breakfast, just like always. He'd had no idea he was going to die that day.

What kind of world did I live in?

* * *

For the first time in my life, I was captivated by grown-up news. In the past I had always found it incredibly boring and avoided it as much as possible. A few years earlier I had been incensed that my usual television cartoons had been preempted for the 1960 Presidential Election results.

Now I followed current events. I was glad to see an arrest had been made of a certain Lee Harvey Oswald, and I was watching the news coverage carefully. That's why I was seated on the floor in front of our black and white TV Sunday while the suspect was being escorted through the Dallas Police Station basement to be transferred to another jail.

I heard a loud bang, and a reporter said, "He's

been shot, he's been shot! Lee Oswald has been shot!"

"Mom," I cried, jumping to my feet. "Someone shot him!"

Mom was in the kitchen. "I know that."

"No! Someone shot Oswald!"

"What?" She dashed into the living room and gazed at the TV.

I stared at the set in wide-eyed wonder.

I had just witnessed someone being murdered, live, on television.

Honestly, what kind of world did I live in?

* * *

As the days passed, I discovered I lived in an evil world full of pain.

Well, I'd already known about being in pain, but the kind Scarlet, et al, inflicted was nothing compared to some of what I saw on the news. I hadn't even been aware of the conflict in Vietnam. I also found out the Soviets were performing tests on nuclear weapons that could blow us to smithereens any second.

Why did people have to be so cruel?

Then, that following February, came a bright spot. The Beatles arrived in New York to be on *The Ed Sullivan Show*.

I had to beg my parents to be allowed to watch the program. Amazingly, Dad consented. I guess he wanted to find out what all the hubbub was about.

But about thirty seconds into "All My Loving" he declared, "That's not music! That's noise!" and switched the channel.

I deflated like a punctured balloon. I should have known better than to even ask.

In the following months, everything was Beatles. Beatles clothing, Beatles wigs, Beatles bubblegum cards, even a Beatles ice cream flavor.

Our school sent home a letter that stated boys were not allowed to have Beatles haircuts but girls were. I seriously thought about asking Mom for one, but it would cost money and would require cropping off my braid, which now reached my waist.

"I," Scarlet announced over a half-eaten green apple one lunch period, "am in love with Paul McCartney. None of the rest of you are allowed to be. You have three other Beatles you can choose from."

Well, with only three, John, George, and Ringo quickly got snatched up by other girls, in that order.

"I'm going to marry Paul someday," Scarlet added.

Verna said, "And I'm going to marry John."

"John's already married," I pointed out.

"You're so stupid," Verna said. "His wife could be dead by the time I'm grown-up."

I did the math in my head. "When you're twenty-one," I said, "John will be thirty-four."

That shut Verna up for a moment. To us, twenty was old. Thirty was ancient.

"Well, he wouldn't even look at someone as ugly as you," Verna sassed.

Like John Lennon was going to be interested in her at ten years old.

8

Scarlet's mom and mine threw us together far too often that summer. I'd learned to swim, so this meant several dreaded trips to the Hansen's kidney-shaped pool. I had to wear a one-piece suit, which of course was an ugly one from a thrift store. It had a pattern of big neon orange and blue squares all over it. Yuck. The other girls, Scarlet, Verna, and Damara, got two-piece bikinis.

Oh, and Mom insisted I wear a swim cap. It was so tight it imprinted red lines on my forehead that were visible when I took it off. A bit too small, it painfully squeezed my head the whole time I was in the pool. But I had to wear it because, according to her, "Otherwise your hair might clog the drain." Funny how Scarlet and her friends got to wear their hair free and their locks wouldn't clog the drain.

I had to endure a lot of kicking, punching, getting shoved from behind into the deep end, and gallons of water splashed in my face. Whenever we played Marco Polo, I was always It, and the other girls would silently steal out of the water and giggle as I thrashed around, trying to find them with my eyes closed.

I knew better than to complain. I'd probably hear something like "They're only teasing!" or "You're far too sensitive!" or "Can't you take a joke?"

Like it was all my fault.

I was so glad when summer vacation ended.

Back to school and Linda!

The first day of fifth grade, I glanced around the room. Linda was nowhere to be seen. Oh, great. *She must be sick again*, I thought. She'd been sick a lot in fourth grade, which was bad for both of us. Bad for Linda because she had to be sick. Bad for me because without her there, I was at the mercy of my tormentors, who, as usual, had no mercy.

This year we girls were allowed one half of the basketball court. Scarlet was out there dribbling at recess and showing off her basketball skills in front of the other girls. I had to admit she was pretty good, swishing the ball through the basket often. Maybe it was because she had a hoop at home, a luxury I wasn't allowed.

I happened to mention Linda's absence.

That stopped the ball play. "Linda's not coming back," Scarlet told me smugly. "She moved away. She probably got tired of looking at your ugly crooked nose."

What?

I mean WHAT?

Linda had moved? And she hadn't told me, her best friend, that she was leaving? But she had told Scarlet? She knew Scarlet hated me!

The basketball thumped twice. "I have her new address," Scarlet bragged.

"Well, may I have it?" I asked. Surely even Scarlet wouldn't deny me that. I thought maybe Linda and I could become pen pals.

She took one deliberate step toward me. "She said not to give it to you."

My lower lip trembled. How could this be happening? Was Scarlet telling the truth? Surely she must be about Linda leaving because it would be all to easily exposed as a lie if Linda showed up the next day. But had Linda given Scarlet her new address? And told her not to let me have it?

As I glanced around at the other girls, I realized it didn't matter if it were the truth or a lie. Everybody now knew Linda had not only abandoned me, she had abandoned me in favor of Scarlet.

That afternoon I ran most of the way home from school and threw myself on my bed, sobbing.

Mom entered the room. "Well, for crying out loud," she said, fists on her hips, "what's the matter with you now? You act like you lost your best friend."

Tears streaming down my face, I sat up. "I did. Linda moved away."

"Well, it's about time you learned that friends will come and go out of your life. You might as well get used to it."

The heel of my hand wiped at my tears. I knew better than to expect any sympathy, but Mom had no idea what the absence of Linda meant.

I had more than lost my best friend.

Without any explanation, my best friend had deserted me.

And thrown me to the wolves.

* * *

You're probably thinking Linda was acting very out of character. I thought so too and, once I stopped weeping, I mentally went back in time, searching for an explanation. We hadn't had a fight. Had I said something wrong? Why, why, why would she just abandon me? Racking my brains produced no answers.

I did find out later there was much more to the story, and if I'd known at the time what was really going on, I would have been even more devastated.

School became a living hell without Linda to protect me. One afternoon in the kitchen while I was setting the table, Mom asked, "Why don't you invite some friends over sometime?"

"I don't have any," I replied.

"Of course you do. You have Scarlet, Verna, and Damara. I know you miss Linda, but she is not the only girl in the world. And you'd have more friends if you'd just be nicer."

As if I were to blame. As if I were deliberately trying to sabotage any friendships.

Well, one recess I tried to make friends with Iona, a mousy little new girl in our class, but she told me "I can't. She'll pick on me too."

"I understand," I told her. Who would volunteer to go through what I was?

And so fifth and sixth grades passed. In the middle of seventh grade, I came home with a report card bound to finally please Dad.

After waiting the obligatory time for a commercial to come on TV, I showed it to him with a flourish.

All A's except for one A-. Surely this time, I thought, I would get some praise.

He immediately zeroed in on the lowest grade. "An A minus in math?" he asked. "Why wasn't that an A?"

I sighed deeply as he signed it. Why wasn't anything ever good enough for my parents?

This time I dared to ask, "What about my other grades?"

Couldn't he see I was pleading for one word of praise? Please, just one word. It wouldn't cost him any money!

He handed the card back to me. "They're okay."

Well, God forbid I should ever get a C! I would probably be grounded until I was fifty!

I wanted to say more, but his television show was starting again. I practically stomped into my room. I wanted to slam the door, but that would only get me into more trouble.

I sat on my bed and mulled over my problem for a few minutes. Couldn't anybody say anything nice about me, ever?

I sighed, but then a smile spread across my face when I came up with a solution.

Great-uncle Mark!

Why hadn't I thought of this before?

I grabbed a pen and tugged out a sheet of the pink stationery Great-uncle Mark had sent me my last birthday.

Dear Great-uncle Mark,

I hope you are doing well.
I got my report card today, and I got all A's

except for an A- in math. But I am trying hard to do better.

I hope you can visit us soon. I would so love to see you!

I had an idea. If you are too busy to visit us, maybe I could come visit you this summer. I know you travel all over the world, so it would be a terrific education for me. Plus, I'd have the joy of spending so much more time with you.

And, I thought but didn't write, *I could get away from Scarlet and her bullying.*

I laid the pen down, slid open a drawer, and found a 3.5" x 5" print of my latest school picture. Great-uncle Mark had asked me to include a photo the next time I wrote him.

Picking up my pen again, I added *Please write me soon and tell me about all the exotic places you are visiting and when I can see you again.*

I love you,

Markette

Mom always insisted on checking my letters before I sent them so, she said, she could make sure the grammar and spelling were correct. I was also totally dependent on her to have Great-uncle Mark's current address. The last I'd heard, he was in Tokyo, working on some financial deal, but he moved around so much I knew that could have changed.

Obediently, I took my letter to Mom in the kitchen. She was dicing an onion, and its pungent scent wafted around the room.

She wiped off her hands and read the letter. "Oh, no," she said. "This will not do. You will not ask to go visit. Great-uncle Mark is a very busy man, and he doesn't need you pestering him when he has important work to do." She handed the letter back to me. "Go fix it."

I hung my head. Of course she wanted me to take out the very best part, the main reason I was sending the letter in the first place. And deleting it meant writing the letter all over again.

But I did. "Now is it okay?" I asked, showing her the revised version.

"Now it's okay. I'll address it, seal it, and put on the postage."

I had just left the kitchen when I turned around and popped my head back in. I was going to ask Mom if she had his current address.

But what I saw was her slipping my class photo out of the envelope.

If you're guessing it's because she didn't want Great-uncle Mark to know my nose was still broken, you are so right. Dad had said they were saving up to get it fixed, but the money always seemed to go for something else, like the transmission on his plumbing truck. Or an upgrade from our black and white TV to a color one.

Knowing my folks, they were too embarrassed to ask for the funds again. I was old enough to understand that message all too well.

Important: My parents' pride. Me: Not so much.

9

One unseasonably hot Saturday afternoon that spring, Mom came home from grocery shopping in a huff. "Markette!" she yelled the moment she stepped into the house.

For crying out loud, *now* what was I in trouble for? I had done my chores—mopping the kitchen floor and vacuuming the entire house. I admit I was more than a bit resentful about it since Scarlet had bragged that she never had to do any housework. No, the Hansens had maid service, so she didn't even have to clean her own bedroom or iron her school blouses like I did.

I had spent what little was left of my time reading in the living room. This was the only space in our house that had a fan. One desk fan oscillating back and forth didn't battle the heat much, but it was better than nothing.

What, I wondered, could I possibly have done to upset her? I set aside *The Fellowship of the Ring* and my visit to Middle Earth. Oh, how I wished I could be swept away to some fantasy land instead of having to live in reality.

"I ran into Evelyn Hansen in the grocery store," Mom said. "She was there to pick up a birthday cake for Scarlet. And she wanted to know why I hadn't RSVP'd your invitation. Why didn't you tell me about her party? Do you have any idea how embarrassed I was?"

Oh. That's right. Today Scarlet was turning thirteen. She'd been gushing about it at school all week, about how she was officially going to be a teenager. But . . .

"I didn't get an invitation," I told Mom. Certainly I was the last person Scarlet wanted at her party.

"Well . . . " Mom said, "maybe it got lost in the mail. But go get dressed! I stopped by the toy store and picked up a gift." She checked her watch. "You better hurry! The party's already starting!"

Oh, great. This was not how I wanted to spend the day. I had a sneaky suspicion Scarlet had sabotaged things so my invitation would deliberately get "lost in the mail."

But what choice did I have? After slipping on my nicest dress, the red one with the white collar, I returned to the kitchen where Mom was putting away the groceries.

"Her present's on the table," Mom said.

I spied a rectangular package enclosed in the free gift wrap our local toy store supplied.

Picking it up, I shook it a bit and heard some rattling inside. "What is it?"

"It's a game. She'll love it. Now get going!"

She practically shooed me out the front door. Of course I was expected to walk, despite the heat. Did I mention how much gas cost? Oh yeah, I did. If I could get anywhere by walking, that was the method of transportation used, unless it was raining. My parents did not see this blazing heat as an obstacle.

But, I consoled myself, an un-airconditioned car

would not have been much better.

I bit my lip as I waited for the light to turn green so I could cross Main Street into the nicer section of town. Was there any way to get out of this party? Out of being bullied all afternoon? The signal changed, and, while strolling to the opposite curb, I dreamed up an idea.

A wonderful idea. An idea so brilliant a light bulb should have popped into existence over my head!

So I was feeling a bit relieved when I rang the Hansen's doorbell.

Mrs. Hansen answered. "Markette! So glad you're here!" She ushered me into the dining room where Scarlet was holding court amidst the other girls from our class, their long oaken table piled high with gifts. One look at me and her eyes first widened with surprise, then narrowed with ire. As I suspected, she had arranged things so I wouldn't show up.

"Um . . . I can't stay," I told Mrs. Hansen. "I just came by to give Scarlet her gift."

Mrs. Hansen glanced at my dress. This had been such an obvious lie, I figured she was not buying it.

"Are you sure? We have cake and ice cream!"

"I have somewhere else I need to be." *Somewhere else I need to be, as in anywhere but here,* I thought.

Another lie, but this one she seemed to believe.

"Well," Mrs. Hansen said, "in that case, Scarlet, why don't you open Markette's gift now so you can thank her in person?"

I handed Scarlet the present, and she, reluctantly, began ripping off the wrapping. I caught a glimpse of the corner of what was inside, and my insides dropped about a mile.

Oh, no! Oh, no no no no no!

NO!

Not the Bandit Buddies game! It said right on the package it was for 3-5 years old.

Oh, I could visualize how this had happened. Mom had been in a big fat hurry, and she had picked up whatever was on the clearance table and therefore cost the least. She would have checked only the price, not anything else about the game.

Scarlet's jaw dropped. "Do you think I'm a baby?" she screeched, slamming the box onto the table.

"Scarlet!" Mrs. Hansen snapped. "Markette came all the way here to give you a gift! You will apologize right now!"

Oh, great. Why, oh why did grown-ups have to involve themselves in these matters, making them a hundred times worse? Scarlet's jaw worked back and forth in an attempt to get those two words out. Having to apologize to *me*, of all people, in front of her friends and classmates was obviously taking considerable effort.

In the meantime, the girls were focused on her. Seconds ticked by. Finally, through gritted teeth she managed a weak "I'm sorry."

It was obviously insincere, but I jumped in to quell the situation. "And I'm sorry I can't stay." I backed toward the front door. "I hope you have a happy birthday."

I was out of there and halfway to the end of the block when footsteps pounded behind me. I turned around.

Scarlet.

She grabbed both of my arms. "You ruined my birthday!" she screamed. "And this is a special birthday, the day I become a teen! My mom is furious. She told me that the moment the party's over, I'm grounded for a week!"

"I'm sorry!" I pleaded. "I didn't know what the gift was. My mother—"

"You think I give a damn?" she interrupted. Her grip on me tightened so hard it hurt. "You know what you are? You're poison! No wonder everybody hates you!"

She shoved me so hard I landed on my rear. I guess even that wasn't enough to vent her rage. Looking down upon me, she spat on my dress.

Shocked, I sat there for a moment while Scarlet dashed back inside and slammed the door.

10

Tears streaked my face. I was crying so hard, I could barely get up.

Once I did rise, I ran. I ran to get away. Feet and heart pounding, I ran across intersections, not even checking to see if they were clear first. I heard the screech of one car's tires, and a nasty "Why don't you look where you're going?" yelled at me.

I didn't care. I just ran.

After a few blocks, I had to slow down. A terrible stitch in my side stabbed my ribs, and I gasped for breath. I stopped, leaning over, hands on my knees. My tears dripping onto the sidewalk quickly evaporated in the sizzling heat.

Eventually I straightened up. My vision was blurry, so I wiped it clear.

What was I supposed to do now?

I couldn't go home. Mom would drive me right back to the party. And somehow I'd get blamed for what had happened. Oh, and have to apologize for it. And definitely get punished for lying and skipping out of the party early.

My big plan had been to drop off the gift then hightail it to the public library which was not only air-conditioned but where I could spend the afternoon reading in peace. Yes, I knew it was a risky move. Yes, I knew Mom might find out about it. But I had figured it would be worth whatever punishment she'd inflict to not only avoid Scarlet but spend some more time in Middle Earth.

My problem now was that the librarian knew Mom, and if I showed up with my eyes red from crying, she was certain to phone her.

And that too would put me right back at the party—along with all those apologies and punishments.

Sunshine, hot as blazes, burned down on me. What was I supposed to do, stand there on the sidewalk for over an hour before going home? My party dress was little protection against the sun's scorching rays.

I glanced around. The sidewalks were deserted. Nobody else was stupid enough to go for a stroll in this sweltering heat. Nary a bird was twittering or soaring through the sky. Even the leaves on the trees were not stirring.

But where could I possibly go?

That's when I saw the bell tower of our church in the distance.

I set off in that direction.

* * *

This may surprise you, but churches used to be open during the day so anyone could come inside, kneel down, and pray.

The heavy back door of my church boomed closed after I stepped inside the narthex. It was thankfully cooler here than outside. I waited a moment for my eyes to adjust to the sudden darkness.

I swung open a door into the nave and glanced around. A couple of people were kneeling in the front pews. Votive candles flickered in their red glass holders. It was blissfully quiet.

I didn't want anybody to see me. I especially didn't want anybody to tell Mom I was there, sobbing.

Then I saw the cry room.

In case you don't know, many Catholic churches have what's called a cry room. It is encased with glass windows, and it's there for parents with noisy babies or small children so their bawling won't disturb the rest of the congregation. It was mostly soundproof.

Perfect. I creaked open the door and stepped inside.

I approached the front window through which I could see the large crucifix over the altar. Christ's head, crowned with thorns, slumped forward in death. Red paint representing blood was on His hands and feet, and a slash was in His side.

Lips blubbering, I sank to the floor in a corner, hugged my legs, and sobbed my heart out.

Well, it was a cry room, wasn't it?

One wave of anguish was replaced by another. Then another. Then another. My ribs ached and my knees were getting wet from my tears.

There was just no way out, I told myself. Life was nothing but useless, pointless pain. And why me? Other people got to find joy and happiness but not me. Was I defective or something? Nobody ever said anything nice about me. Everybody told me I was ugly and stupid, so it must be true.

And there wasn't anything I could do about it.

A fly I must have let in buzzed around me. I

swatted at it, but it kept hounding me, sometimes landing next to my ear. Stupid fly! Why did it have to pester me? Wasn't I suffering enough already?

Finally I stopped weeping. I had no more.

Head down, I just sat there.

That's when a voice said, "Are you all right?"

My head jerked up. The cry room's door was squeaky, but I hadn't heard anyone open it.

The voice had come from a brown-haired boy, about my age, seated on the front pew. He wore jeans, a white T-shirt, and tennis shoes.

"I'm fine," I told him.

An obvious lie.

"You don't look fine," he said. "What's wrong?"

"Nothing."

"Something's wrong. My name's Joshua. What's yours?"

Remember that I told you we'd get to the most important character in the story eventually? It may not seem like it, but this is the guy. If you keep reading, I think you'll find it was worth the wait.

I was silent for a moment. Then I said, "Markette," even though I'd had no intention of telling him.

"Well, Markette," he said, rising, stepping to me, and leaning over to grasp my hands, "why don't you sit with me and tell me all about this nothing that's wrong?"

Maybe, I thought, as he helped me up, it would be good to talk it out. I settled on the pew beside him.

"Everybody hates me."

"God doesn't hate you."

"Okay, but everybody else does. Well, except my Great-uncle Mark. I don't have any friends, and I can't do anything to please my parents."

Joshua leaned back a bit. "Is that why you're crying right now, here in church? Something bad must have happened today."

"Scarlet happened."

"Who's that?"

"The world's biggest bully! She picks on me all the time! She even goes looking for reasons to hurt me! She's—"

"—a child of God, created in His own image and likeness," Joshua finished for me.

I blinked in surprise. C'mon, admit it. You were surprised he said that too, weren't you?

I soon recovered from my astonishment. "Well, she doesn't always act like a child of God."

"Do you always act like a child of God?"

I gazed at my lap. "Well, no," I admitted, glancing up. Then I pointed at my nose. "But you see this nose? She did this!"

"This nose?" Joshua asked, touching it with his thumb and index finger.

I was about to swat his hand away when he removed it himself.

He rose and stared through the glass window at the crucifix above the altar. "Did you know the Christ was bullied?"

I stood next to him and stared at the crucifix too. What a weird way to refer to Jesus, as *the* Christ.

"I never saw it that way," I said.

"The Pharisees came all the way out from Jerusalem to mock Him while He was hanging in utter agony."

That's right. I had read about that in the Bible.

The fly started zipping around my face again. I waved my arms, trying to shoo it away.

"And there were flies," Joshua added. "During the crucifixion, there were flies."

My first thought was *What a weird thing to say!* But as I mused about it further, I realized it must have been true. All the blood and sweat surely would have drawn flies, especially in a day and age of poor hygiene.

I have to tell you this hit me like a ton of bricks. The mental image of Jesus with flies buzzing around His sacred head and crawling on the crown of thorns made the crucifixion suddenly REAL. He couldn't swat them away, oh no. Surely it had been the least of His sufferings, but this image made it present, like it was happening right now, instead of some historical event two thousand years ago.

"I know He died for our sins," I said. "But why did they want to crucify Him?"

Joshua turned to face me. "They were envious."

"Are you sure?"

"It's in the Bible."

I looked it up later, and he was right. Matthew 27:18 and Mark 15:10.

"Bullies," he stated, "bully out of envy."

What? Was he suggesting Scarlet was jealous of me? That was ridiculous!

Scarlet was the one with the beautiful red hair in

a ponytail, with the big two-story air-conditioned house, with the swimming pool, with lots of money, with maid service, with parents who pretty much let her do whatever she wanted.

What did I have? Nothing!

But Joshua wasn't done. "The Christ forgave them. Have you forgiven Scarlet?"

I'm ashamed to say it had not even occurred to me to forgive her.

I gazed at the floor a moment.

When I looked up, Joshua was gone.

11

Frantically I glanced around the cry room. How had Joshua gotten out so quickly? I hadn't heard the door creak, and it practically groaned when I slipped out and checked if he was in the narthex.

No sign of him anywhere.

Okay, that was just plain weird.

I re-entered the nave and glimpsed the clock above the exit. It was late enough that I could walk home.

While putting one foot in front of the other, I thought about what Joshua had said. Forgive Scarlet? After all, didn't I pray "Forgive us our trespasses *as* we forgive those who trespass against us"? So I guess I had to, but I shuddered to think what evils she would have planned for me at school this Monday.

When I arrived home, Dad was watching sports on our new color TV. Apparently, the upgrade from a black and white television was somehow more important than getting my nose fixed, but Dad was insistent that he wanted to watch *Star Trek* and *Bonanza* in color.

As usual I had to crawl beneath his line of sight. This was tougher to do than before because this was a console TV, and the screen was closer to the floor. Somehow I managed to wiggle through.

From the kitchen Mom asked, "How was the party?"

Well, what was I supposed to say to that?

"Okay, I guess," I mumbled noncommittedly.

"Come set the table for dinner."

Obligingly, I got the plates. I had just placed them onto the table and turned to get the glasses when Mom, gazing at me, gasped, "What happened to your nose?"

What? Oh, no! Something else was wrong with it? I covered it with both hands. No, no, no! Could this day get any worse?

"Harold!" Mom called. "Come take a look at Markette!"

"Wait for a commercial!" Dad shouted.

"No! Now! It's important!"

He did not make an appearance in the kitchen. After a few moments, to my utter shock, Mom stomped into the living room, grabbed the remote, and shut off the TV.

"You need to see this NOW!"

Lips tight, Dad slammed the leg-rest of his recliner shut. He stood.

"This better be import—" was as far as he got when Mom tugged my hands aside to reveal my nose.

Dad's eyes widened. "It's straight!"

What? My nose was fixed?

"How did that happen?" he added.

"I . . . I . . ."

"What happened at that party?" Mom demanded.

"Uh . . . " How was I supposed to explain this when I didn't know the answer myself? Wait. Could Joshua have had something to do with it? He had touched my nose, after all.

"Um . . . after I left the party, I walked over to the church," I began.

Mom frowned. "Why did you go to the church?"

"Isn't it okay for me to drop by the church to pray?" Notice how careful I was not to tell a lie. I hadn't said that's why I went there. I merely asked if it were okay to go there for that purpose.

"Well, yes," Mom said, "but you're not saying you asked for a miracle, are you?"

"No. There was this boy there—"

That was as far as I got. Both of my parents zeroed in on the word *boy*.

"What boy?" Dad snapped. "Who is this boy?"

"Is he someone from your school?" Mom asked.

I shrugged. "I'd never seen him before. He touched my nose—"

"You mean to tell me," Mom interrupted, her eyes wide, "that you let some strange boy touch you?"

"I didn't ask him to. He just did." I shrugged again. "I guess he popped it back into place? That's all I know."

"Well, I'll be," Dad said. "That kid has saved us a pile of money. I'm getting the camera. We're sending a picture of this to Uncle Mark right away."

Now you think my mother would have been happy about this, right?

What I got instead was "For crying out loud, why didn't you tell us all you needed to do was pop it back into place?"

Like I knew that. Like a kid would know that

when an adult didn't, when even the doctor didn't.

If I'd known that, wouldn't I have popped it back into place myself a long time ago?

"I want to see it," I begged.

"Go take a look," Mom said.

Never had I scurried so fast into another room. *Wow,* I thought, gazing into the bathroom mirror. It looked terrific! I ran my finger down the bridge. Straight!

How had Joshua done it? I didn't see how he could have, but he was the only one who had touched it, so . . .

Who was this kid Joshua anyway?

What was he?

I hoped I would see him again. I wanted to thank him.

Dad ordered me into the living room for the photo.

I grinned from ear to ear as the flashcube temporarily blinded me.

* * *

That Monday morning I was waiting to cross Elm Avenue on my way to school when I heard a familiar voice behind me.

"Hey, Crook Nose!"

Scarlet. Of course. Here to exact her revenge for what had happened at the birthday party.

This time I had more confidence. I turned around and stated plainly, "Are you talking to me?"

Boy, did her eyes widen! Boy, did her jaw drop! Verna and Damara had similar looks on their faces.

The signal turned green and I started across the

street. They just stood there, thunderstruck.

"Aren't you coming?" I asked.

Amazingly, they walked several paces behind me all the way to school.

* * *

School was buzzing with the news about my nose. The fact that it was straight was as plain as . . . well, as plain as the nose on my face.

During recess I decided to return the school library's copy of *The Fellowship of the Ring*. I'd finished it Sunday and was looking forward to the next book in *The Lord of the Rings* trilogy.

I checked out *The Two Towers* and debated about whether or not to start reading it immediately or go to recess in the girls' yard.

Well, that wasn't too difficult a decision to make since I figured Scarlet was still set on tormenting me with some kind of revenge.

I settled down in a rather ratty brown chair someone who didn't want it anymore had donated to the school. It was in something of a cubby hole in a corner, a perfect place to peacefully read for the next ten minutes or so.

Amid the musty smell of hundreds of library books, I turned the cover into a new adventure. I had immersed myself for only a few pages when I heard three familiar voices behind the stacks: Scarlet, Verna, and Damara. I froze, listening and hoping they wouldn't come this way and see me. By sitting in a corner, I was, well, cornered.

Damara said, "What do you suppose happened?"

"Well, she must have seen a doctor," Verna answered. "Maybe that's why she left the party early, because she had a doctor's appointment."

"I can't believe this," Scarlet grumbled. "Already she was the prettiest girl in school, and look at her now!"

I'm sure my eyes were never so wide as they were when I heard that. What? They thought I was pretty? They always told me I was ugly! I had come to believe it myself. Hey, when everybody tells you you're stupid and ugly, after a while you start to believe it.

"You can tell she's going to be really beautiful when she grows up," Verna added.

"This is so unfair!" Scarlet snarled. "She's pretty, she's smart..."

I'm smart? I wondered, almost gasping out loud. The way Dad had gone on about my grades, I had figured everybody else got grades like mine or better.

"... and you know what else?" Scarlet griped. "You ever hear of Mark Mason?"

Whoa! What was this about Great-uncle Mark?

"The gazillionaire?" Damara asked. "The one who plays golf with President Johnson?"

"Yeah," Scarlet said. "Him. My mom told me Markette's related to him. She was even named after him! He's the one who pays for her tuition here."

"Really?" Verna and Damara gasped in unison.

"Her dad is his only relative, so guess who's getting all that money when he dies. And guess who will get it later when her dad dies."

"Oh, my gosh," Damara said. "Markette's going to be filthy rich?"

I was going to be wealthy? I had not even realized that. But I didn't want Great-uncle Mark's money. I wanted Great-uncle Mark.

"I hate her," Scarlet snarled. "I hate her so much. She gets it all. She gets looks, and smarts, and money. And she hasn't done anything to deserve any of it."

The bell ending recess trilled.

I heard them shuffle out of the library.

Stunned, I sat there in that ratty brown chair, the open book on my lap. I couldn't believe what I had just overheard.

Joshua had been right.

They bullied me because they were envious.

The question was: What was I going to do with this new information?

12

Well, one thing this new information was going to do for me was inspire a lot of confidence. Now I knew that when Scarlet called me names, those words were springing out of jealousy. And, considering what had happened at her birthday party, and what I had overheard in the library, I knew she would come after me at lunchtime.

But first, when we arrived in the schoolyard, amid the thumping of balls from the nearby basketball court, the other girls in the class gathered around me to check out the new shape of my nose. Even some of the boys, who had come into the yard to use the drinking fountain, wanted to examine it.

That's where we girls were, next to the volleyball court. Seventh grade girls got half a volleyball court. I don't know what we were supposed to do with only half a court, but that's where Scarlet volleyed her assault.

"Hey, stupid!" I heard as she drew up behind me. Well, I knew she wasn't going to call me Crook Nose any more. "Your nose may be better, but you're still ugly!"

I turned around. "So . . . you're superior to me?"

Her eyes widened. She probably couldn't believe how easy I was making this for her.

"You bet I am!"

"And I'm inferior to you."

"That's right!"

"And it's obvious to everybody? Really, really

obvious?"

"It sure is! Even more obvious than your stupid nose!"

"Well," I said, turning to the other girls, "she must think you're incredibly stupid. It's obvious she's superior and I'm inferior, but she has to keep proving it to you over and over and over again. Or maybe . . . "

I laid a finger on my cheek. "Maybe, just maybe, she doesn't really think she's such hot stuff but wants you to believe it."

Iona tittered. A few of the others followed suit. Scarlet blushed red as the titters evolved into giggles.

"That's not true!" Scarlet shrieked.

"Isn't it?" I asked. "If it isn't, why is your face turning red?"

She stomped away. From a lunch table, she glared at me.

If looks could kill, I would have been dead a hundred times, but I didn't care.

Iona high-fived me. "It's about time somebody took her down."

* * *

After school, I stopped by the church. I wanted to thank God for my nose being fixed. I also wanted to avoid running into Scarlet and her buddies on the way home. A confrontation on the playground with a lot of other girls around was one thing. Having to deal with those bullies alone on a city street was another.

As usual, the church was blessedly silent, the

flames of votive candles colored red by their crimson glass holders. I couldn't believe my luck. Joshua was there, sitting in a pew way in the back. I slid in next to him.

"Hi, Markette," he said.

"Hi, Joshua. I want to thank you for fixing my nose. That was you, wasn't it?"

"God fixed it," he said simply.

"Wait'll I tell you what happened today." Quickly I outlined what had occurred in the library and at lunchtime. I wound up the story by saying, "And Scarlet finally got what's coming to her. I totally humiliated her in front of everybody!"

Joshua sat back a bit. "So," he said, "now *you're* the bully?"

Talk about bursting my bubble. Deflating my balloon. Knocking down my house of cards. Stomping on my sandcastle. I'd come up with more metaphors, but you get the idea. Here I had thought Joshua would grin and say something like "You really showed her! Good for you!"

C'mon, admit it. When you read what had happened in the playground, you were thinking something like that yourself, weren't you?

"She deserved it," I pointed out, trying to justify myself. "It's about time she got a taste of her own medicine."

"And you've appointed yourself the doctor who's going to prescribe it for her? Isn't that God's job? Doesn't He say 'Revenge is mine, I will repay'"?

I slumped in my seat on the pew. "Yes. But

what else was I supposed to do?"

"What were you supposed to do? Didn't the Christ say to love your enemies and do good to those who persecute you?"

"Look," I said, pointing a finger at him. "Why does a loving God even allow stuff like this to happen? Doesn't He have any idea how much I've been suffering?"

"I think God knows all about suffering," Joshua said, once again staring at the crucifix above the altar. "But don't you believe God can bring good out of evil? Isn't that what the Christ's sacrifice on the cross did? And aren't you supposed to be sacrificial like Him?"

"I suppose so."

"By the way, have you forgiven Scarlet yet?"

"Um . . . I haven't exactly gotten around to it."

Joshua's brown eyes were soft. "And how about apologizing for humiliating her this afternoon? How about apologizing to her in front of the girls who witnessed what you did?"

My jaw dropped and I flung up my arms. "This," I grumbled, "is not fair. I finally get the best of Scarlet, and you're telling me I should apologize to her for it? I'm always having to apologize to Scarlet! And for things I didn't even do!"

"But this time it's something you did do."

I admit I started whining. "No. I'm sick of being a doormat. I'm sick of always getting stomped on. I'm sick of being the one who doesn't have any power or say in what happens."

"You want to be the powerful one?" Joshua

asked. "How much power do you think it would take to make an apology like that?"

I squeezed my eyes shut. Unbidden in my mind played a scene from the crucifixion: *In like manner also the chief priests mocking, said with the scribes one to another: He saved others; himself he cannot save. Let Christ the king of Israel come down now from the cross, that we may see and believe. And they that were crucified with him reviled him.*

He could have, I realized. He could have come down from the cross. Jesus was the most powerful human being who ever lived. He could multiply loaves and fishes. He could walk on water. He could heal the blind and the sick.

He was God, after all. Omnipotent. Coming down from the cross would have been easy. Putting a stop to all the pain and suffering would have been a snap.

And He could have shown up those obnoxious bullies with one simple action.

Can you imagine what would have happened if He really had come down from the cross? Those conceited snobs who had been jeering Him just seconds ago would have slammed to their knees—no, planted their faces in the dirt—and been screaming for mercy.

Boy, would He have shown them!

I bit my tongue. It was kind of like what I had done to Scarlet. I . . . well, hadn't I in a sense come down off the cross she'd erected for me? Hadn't I really shown her?

But, as I thought about it, didn't it take more

power, more self-will, more self-control for Jesus to continue hanging in agony? To endure the mockery? When *every single second* was another moment He had chosen not to put an end to it?

I would hardly call Jesus a doormat. It had been His decision to lay down His life. Nobody took it from Him.

If I were going to be Christ-like . . .

I sighed, deeply. I too had a decision to make.

Was I going to pick up this, my cross, and follow Him? Or was I going to fling my cross aside?

My hand closed around the cross Great-uncle Mark had given me.

When I opened my eyes, Joshua was gone.

* * *

I sweat bullets Tuesday morning. During recess I couldn't summon up the courage to apologize to Scarlet. I wanted to wait until after school on the way home where I would have more privacy, but Joshua was right. It should happen in front of all the girls.

So that afternoon, when I and my classmates arrived outside with our lunches, I announced, "I have something to say in front of everyone."

Scarlet gazed at me slant-eyed. I'm sure she was expecting more of what I'd given her the day before.

I turned to her as our female classmates gathered around. "I want to apologize to Scarlet for what I said yesterday. It wasn't right, and I'm sorry."

I admit I was mostly sorry about humiliating myself by saying all that.

Scarlet, lips contorted in smugness, walked up to me with deliberation, right into my personal space. "I do *not* accept your apology." She grabbed my sack lunch out of my hands and tossed it to Verna, who tossed it to Damara.

Thus began a game of keep-away, I tried to grab it back, but the three of them were taller than me. Eventually Scarlet lobbed my lunch over her head and right into the school dumpster.

"Oops."

I stared at the dumpster, at flies buzzing and zigzagging above it. The stench from inside was putrid, mostly from discarded milk cartons.

I should have known something like this would happen.

Maybe this time I deserved it.

13

I wanted to tell Joshua how badly the apology had gone and about how Scarlet had thrown away my lunch, but he wasn't there when I visited the church after school. Nor was he there the next day, nor the next.

I wasn't being called stupid or ugly anymore, but Scarlet and company were grabbing my lunch, prying it out of my hands if necessary, and flinging it into the dumpster on a daily basis. This was worse than being called names. All I was getting at noon was the pint of milk Great-uncle Mark had paid for, and that was only because I managed to drink it before I got to the lunch tables. I was going hungry!

By Friday, I'd had enough. Didn't I deserve justice? And this wasn't just about me. My parents had worked hard to provide my lunch every day. So, despite my vow never to again ask an adult for help with my bullies, I complained to our principal, Sister Angela, who was also the eighth-grade teacher. She called the four of us, Scarlet, Verna, Damara, and me, into her office.

Sister Angela was in her mid-forties and had the straightest teeth I had ever seen. "Have you three girls been throwing away Markette's lunch?" she asked from behind her desk.

I have to give Scarlet credit for one thing. She had her wide-eyed innocent look down pat. "Absolutely not! Markette has been throwing her lunches into the dumpster herself. She said she hates the lunches her mom makes, that she's sick to death of peanut butter."

"Verna, is this true?" Sister asked.

Scarlet must have given Verna lessons in fake innocence because her mouth was open in a counterfeit shock. "Yes, Sister! And Markette is always trying to get Scarlet into trouble. That's why she's accusing her!"

Sister Angela's eyebrows rose. "Markette, should I call your mother and ask her about this?"

I stared at the floor. "No." What was the point? History told me Mom would believe Scarlet over her own daughter any day.

Only after I said it did I realize my "No" could have been taken as an admission of guilt.

"You will eat whatever your mother packs for your lunch," Sister Angela admonished.

I sighed. "Yes, Sister."

She dismissed the other girls but told me to stay behind. I swallowed, hard. I just knew I was going to be punished, yet again, for something Scarlet had done.

But Sister was wiser than I'd thought. "I don't know what's really going on here," she said. "But I have heard reports of bullying on the playground. And I've heard you've been the victim of it several times. But unless I have some proof . . . "

I glanced up. "And it's the word of the three of them against the one of me."

"Exactly. I did speak to some of the other girls in your class, but they didn't see what happened."

Of course that's what they'd said, even though

they had witnessed all of it. They didn't want to lose their lunches either.

"I'm sorry," Sister said, "but my hands are tied."

* * *

I understand that in your century you've got phones that will do just about anything in addition to phone calls. You can actually carry them around in a pocket and use them as flashlights, as cameras, and recorders.

Oh, how I would have loved having something like that so I could get the proof I needed! Imagine if I'd been able to play a recording, especially a video one, of Scarlet stealing my lunch.

Well, we did have audio tape recorders back then, but they were mostly big clumsy things. Check on the internet for images of tape recorders from old episodes of the television show *Mission Impossible*, and you'll see what I mean. Even a cassette recorder wasn't something I could stealthily use, even if I'd had one.

Which I didn't.

Monday morning I left for school early, as usual hoping to avoid Scarlet and her constant yanking of my braid. Walking down Main Street, I passed our local supermarket and a couple of bars.

That's when I saw him—an old man sitting on a crate in an alley between stores. I'd seen him out of the corner of my eye before, but, like most people, I'd ignored him. He was not the sort of person a thirteen-year-old girl would want to approach. His clothes—jeans and an old T-shirt—were dirty and ratty, hanging on a thin, bony frame. His gray hair and beard were so unkempt they looked like they hadn't been attended to in months, if not years. Eyes were rheumy, and a trembling hand was extended, palm up, as he begged.

Flies buzzed around him, some crawling on his skin. They reminded me of the flies I'd envisioned around Jesus during the crucifixion and also the flies over the dumpster at school. For all I knew, those flies were getting my food instead of me.

As I glanced down at the sack lunch perched on my schoolbooks, then back up at him, I remembered Joshua saying *Don't you believe God can bring good out of evil? Isn't that what the Christ's sacrifice on the cross did? And aren't you supposed to be sacrificial like Him?*

I debated with myself for a moment, then asked him, "Are you hungry?"

Staring at me, he nodded.

"You like bologna? With mustard?"

Despite my requests, Mom didn't always give me peanut butter.

He nodded again.

Well, why not? I wasn't going to get to eat it anyway.

I approached and was almost overwhelmed by a stench emanating from him. He obviously hadn't bathed for days, maybe weeks.

"You can have this," I said, holding out the sack far enough for him to reach it while I still managed to keep back as much as possible.

Without a word, he snatched it and peered inside.

As I walked away, I glanced over my shoulder.

He was cramming the sandwich into his mouth as fast as he could.

* * *

Remember what I told you about how I had originally planned to head for the library after leaving Scarlet's birthday party so I could avoid her bullying?

Well, the city wasn't the only place with a library, of course. That day I gulped down my milk the moment I got outside for lunch, then headed straight back inside where I could spend my lunchtime reading. We weren't allowed to bring food into the library, but what food did I have anyway?

I'd finished *The Two Towers* and was looking forward to *The Return of the King* so I could complete Tolkien's Ring Trilogy. Besides, the library had another advantage as a place to spend my free time: during lunch the principal, Sister Angela, worked a half-hour shift there at the circulation desk until Sister Thomas came in and took over for her. I was not only away from Scarlet but if anything happened there, I would have a witness.

Grinning, I found the book I wanted and settled down in that ratty brown chair. I could just envision Scarlet wondering why I wasn't at the lunch tables with the rest of the girls. She was, I thought, probably frantically searching for me.

Yeah, I knew she'd eventually figure it out, but in the meantime I'd get some quality reading time in addition to some peace and quiet.

Well, peace and quiet except for my stomach occasionally rumbling with hunger.

* * *

Weeks passed and we were soon approaching June and the end of seventh grade. Sure enough, Scarlet did find me in the library, but I merely winked at her as if to say *What are you going to do to me here?*

She'd left in a huff.

I was daily giving my lunch to the homeless man and learning to subsist on the sole pint of milk I got. I was also checking the church after school to see if by chance Joshua was there. I was always disappointed, but I started taking some time to pray anyway. I told Mom about my visits so she wouldn't worry. She didn't look too happy about me coming home late all the time, but she could hardly forbid me from slipping into church and praying.

I was beginning to worry what the beggar man was going to do for food once summer vacation started.

Then Dad changed the entire situation.

In a way, he made it worse, a lot worse.

But in a way he ended up making it better, even though that was hardly his intent.

It started one evening when he came home from work. He took one step inside the house and bellowed, "Markette!"

I'd been reading in my bedroom, but he was so loud that I about jumped out of my skin. Uh oh. What had I done now?

I scurried to the living room so his rage wouldn't build while waiting for me. "What?" I asked.

Mom, eyes wide, stepped in from the kitchen. "What's going on?"

Dad's face was red with fury. "Did you give your lunch to a wino? Don't bother lying because I saw you."

"What's this?" Mom gasped.

An accusing finger pointed at me. "I was driving down Main in my truck, and I saw your daughter handing her lunch to some old wino."

Oh, this was bad, very bad. The fact that Dad had divorced himself from being my father by telling Mom I was *her* daughter instead of his, well, that meant he was steamed beyond belief.

But was that man a wino? I hadn't seen any liquor bottles around him, and I also hadn't seen the typical paper bag hiding a bottle.

How could I explain what I had done? I knew I shouldn't just give away the lunch my parents provided me, but since Scarlet would have tossed it into the trash, I wasn't going to get to eat it anyway.

But they wouldn't believe that.

"He was hungry," I pleaded. "He's a child of God, created in His own image and likeness."

"I," Dad stated like he hadn't even heard me, "do not go out and work hard every day to earn money for food so you can hand it to some old wino! How long has this been going on?"

Um, I hadn't counted the days. I hedged a bit. "A while."

Mom's lips were tight. "I've been making lunch

for some bum? A bum who can't even bother to get a"—and she spelled it out for emphasis—"J-O-B?"

I stared at the floor. What else could I say to abate their fury?

Nothing.

"Well," Dad said, "since you don't like the food around here, no dinner for you tonight. You will go to your room and stay there until tomorrow, thinking about what you've done. And nothing to eat until breakfast!" More words followed me as I slunk down the hall. "And you are never to give away your lunch again! Do you hear me?"

I threw myself on my bed and cried. It was bad enough I was in trouble and getting hungrier by the moment, but what about the old man? How hungry was he going to get?

After a while I sat up and thought about what Dad had said. I was to 1) stay in my room until tomorrow, 2) have nothing to eat until breakfast, and 3) think about what I had done.

The thinking is what inspired an idea.

That night after my parents went to bed, I waited, watching the clock on my nightstand, until one minute after midnight. It was officially the next day, and I was therefore allowed to leave my room.

Quietly I stole into the kitchen and grabbed a couple of knives.

14

I just realized you might be thinking the reason I stole into the kitchen to get some knives was because I was planning on doing my parents in.

No, not at all. For one thing, it would have been downright impossible to do that with these knives. One was a regular butter knife, the kind you normally use when eating dinner. The other was a white plastic one. The latter I got out of a box of cutlery left over from a party years ago.

And for another thing, I had a completely different plan for these knives.

The refrigerator was humming, and I admit I was tempted to grab something out of it to eat. I was simply starving, but I stayed obedient to my parents.

After returning to my room, I stashed the plastic knife with my schoolbooks. The other I inserted into the slot of my piggybank.

Iona at school had told me one way to get money out of a piggybank was to stick a knife into the slot, turn the whole thing upside-down, and shake the bank. This would cause the coins to bump up against the knife and turn in the right direction to fall out.

Mentally I crossed my fingers that this would work. A couple of shakes later, I was rewarded with a quarter silently plopping onto my mattress. More jostling rewarded me with another fifty cents. I kept at it until I had a few dollars' worth.

* * *

That morning I wolfed down my cereal and practically zoomed out the front door. I was on a mission.

"You make sure you eat all your lunch!" Mom bellowed after her usual warning not to step in any ink.

"I'll do my best!" I shouted back as I scurried down the driveway. What more could I promise?

When I approached the old man on Main Street, he expectantly held out his hand for his regular daily meal.

"I'm sorry," I told him, "but my father says I can't give you my lunch anymore."

Oh, that poor man! He put his head in both hands and sobbed uncontrollably.

"Don't cry!" I assured him. "Dad said I couldn't give you my lunch, but he didn't say I couldn't buy you some food."

The man glanced up, probably only then noticing I was carrying two paper sacks. One held my lunch. The other was from the supermarket on the previous block.

I glanced around to make sure Dad's truck was nowhere in sight. "I got you a loaf of bread and a jar of peanut butter along with a plastic knife so you can make lots of sandwiches. I also got you a pint of milk and a surprise too!"

The surprise was a Hershey bar tucked into the bottom of the paper bag.

I'd had to hurry in the supermarket to get these things without being late for school. I figured peanut butter didn't have to be refrigerated, and a jar along with a loaf of bread would keep this guy fed for a few days, at least.

Besides, who didn't like peanut butter? Despite what Scarlet had told Sister Angela, I loved it.

I enjoyed my own sandwich on the way to school. After all, I had promised my mother I would eat it.

* * *

That summer I often told my folks I was walking over to the church to pray. One reason was that I was still keeping an eye out for Joshua. Since I didn't see him, eventually I figured he had probably moved away like Linda had. Another reason was trips to the supermarket. I hoped Mom wouldn't notice the amount in my piggybank was depleting, but she never checked. Bread was 22¢ a loaf, so one took up almost an entire quarter. Peanut butter was more, and I did try to get the old man some milk from time to time.

I scoured the city for soda bottles to supplement the little money I had. If I found two, the man got a candy bar for dessert and I had a penny left to help buy something else the next time.

I should mention I was also praying at the church, like I had told my parents. I was there on my knees way in the back one summer day when guess who showed up?

Okay, you don't have to guess, do you?

"Where have you been?" I whispered.

"Oh, I'm always around," Joshua said, kneeling beside me. "So, have you forgiven Scarlet yet?"

We sat in the pew. "I've tried. It's so hard to do.

I forgive her but then she does something else to me."

That was true. Summer visits to the Hansen's pool hadn't improved at all. Every time water was splashed in my face or I was shoved into the deep end, I tried to remind myself that Jesus could have come down from the cross but hadn't—and that's where the power lay.

It helped a bit, but sometimes it was so hard not to lash out. It was especially hard not to blab about what I had overheard in the library that fateful day after my nose had been fixed and let those nasty bullies know I was fully aware that they were picking on me out of envy.

I added, "It's difficult to forgive someone when what she's done still hurts."

"Have you tried rejoicing?" Joshua asked.

My jaw dropped. "Rejoicing? At being hurt?" Was this kid nuts or something?

"St. Paul rejoiced in his sufferings because he knew good would come out of them," Joshua said. "It's in the Bible. Colossians 1:24."

He sat back in the pew, his mood suddenly very serious. "What if God could make all kinds of good come out of your sufferings? What if your pain could help a lot of children who are in worse pain than you? Would that make it worthwhile?"

I frowned. "Well, yes. But that's not possible." Honestly, how could such a thing happen? How could that kind of good come out of me being bullied?

"Nothing is impossible for God," Joshua said.

"Light can overcome darkness, but darkness cannot overcome light." He stared me in the eye, hands clasped with both index fingers straight up before his lips. "What if your death could help a lot of children? Would that be worth dying for? Would you be willing to make that kind of sacrifice?"

At first what he said scared me so much my lower lip trembled. Then, in my mind's eye, I saw a vision of a beautiful field with lilies scattered about, thousands and thousands of them in a variety of colors: patches of white, red, yellow, orange and pink. Somehow the flowers transformed into children, battered and bruised, their arms straining toward me, begging for help.

I blinked, and the vision faded. *What was that?* I wondered.

"Would so many be worth dying for?" Joshua asked, as though he had seen it too.

I stared deeply into his brown eyes. They held a seriousness I hadn't seen before. Was he actually asking me if I would really die for such children?

A deep breath filled my lungs. I swallowed hard, then made up my mind.

"Yes," I said. "They would be worth dying for."

I meant it, too. They truly would be, although I didn't see how such a thing was possible.

As I gazed at the crucifix over the altar, my hand grasped the golden cross Great-uncle Mark had given me. Dying to help others was, after all, what Jesus had done, and wasn't I supposed to be Christ-like?

I had told myself that if Joshua ever showed up

again, I would keep my eye on him every second so he couldn't disappear on me.

But this one distraction was enough to let him slip away.

15

Once I was fourteen, I was allowed to babysit. My mother wouldn't let me charge more than 50¢ an hour, 75¢ past midnight. I was happy to have even that much minding the two unruly boys who lived down our street. Buying food for the old man was severely depleting the amount in my piggybank.

"I charge $2 an hour babysitting," I overheard Scarlet brag before class began one day. "And I get it too."

Yeah, she probably did. I wished I did. Babysitting, the weekly quarter for my allowance, plus the return of soda bottles wasn't enough to feed a grown man, even if I mostly bought bread and peanut butter. I had to hold my breath every time my mother entered my room. I was so afraid she'd pick up my piggybank and notice it didn't weigh anything like it should.

In the meantime surely you don't think Scarlet had turned over a new leaf and decided to leave me alone.

It was more than a little nerve-racking wondering what she was planning. But what could she do? I was spending my recesses and lunch hours in the library. Either Sister Angela or Sister Thomas was there the whole time, although occasionally Sister Thomas was late showing up so Sister Angela could get her lunch. Sometimes she forgot and didn't show up at all.

So of course it was on one of those occasions when Sister Thomas was absent that Scarlet and her minions decided to make their move.

Sister Angela had been nervously checking her watch every few minutes. No Sister Thomas. Finally she asked, "Markette, will you watch the desk for a few minutes?" The library was empty expect for me, so I'm sure she thought it would be all right.

I rose from my chair in the cubby. "Sure, Sister."

Scarlet and her minions must have been loitering in the classroom hall, waiting for just this opportunity. The moment Sister closed the door to the Faculty Lounge, probably for an urgent bathroom break, Scarlet and Verna streamed into the library while Damara stayed behind as a lookout. The two of them started knocking books off the shelves.

"Stop!" I cried.

"Oh, my goodness, Markette, what are you doing?" Scarlet sassed. "Shame on you knocking all these books to the floor."

The two of them managed to sweep off an entire stack before Damara entered the room, signaling them to stop.

Upon her return, Sister's jaw dropped at the sight. "What happened here?"

All three pointed at me.

As if Sister would believe that. As if I'd had enough time to knock so many books down.

"The moment we came in here," Scarlet said, "Markette said she was going to get us into trouble.

Then she started doing this."

"Markette?"

Just then the bell ending lunch rang.

From deep inside myself, I summoned up my courage.

"I'll come in after school and put them back up," I said.

"Thank you, Markette. As for the three of you," she added, gazing at my bullies, "don't think for one moment I don't know who's really responsible."

But as usual, there was no proof . . .

. . . not even the smirk on Scarlet's face as she sashayed out of the room.

* * *

During this eighth-grade year I knocked myself out studying. I was not going to have Dad complain about an A- ever again.

And guess what? All the work paid off! Halfway through the year I had a straight A report card!

Now, wouldn't you be *thrilled* to bring one of those home? If you're a parent, wouldn't you gush with jubilation if your kid earned those grades?

This time I was bouncing on my toes with excitement while waiting for Dad's TV show to go to commercial. Finally, an ad for Virginia Slims cigarettes came on. This brand was being advertised as smokes just for women.

Grinning, I flourished my report card in front of him.

His eyebrows rose.

In delight, I hoped.

So here it would come. That one word of praise.

Okay, you probably already know that's not what I got. This was a perfect report card, but you've never met my dad.

"No A+?" he asked. "Not even one? I would expect you to get at least one."

Oh, come on! "Dad, Sister Angela doesn't give A+s."

He scribbled his signature on it. "She would if you asked her."

I hung my head and, shoulders slumped, headed to my room.

While I was sitting on the bed, my eyes narrowed. I imagined Mom and Dad dying and going up to the Pearly Gates. There St. Peter welcomed them in—I mean I figured as awful as they were to me, they'd still get there—and showed them around Heaven. At the end of the tour, he asked "Don't you love it? Isn't Heaven perfect?"

And Mom said, "Well . . . it would be better if you put this over here."

And Dad added, "And if you put that over there."

Because even perfection wasn't perfect enough for them.

Yeah, I know. That was silly. It would never happen.

But thinking about it did make me feel a bit better.

* * *

The next day after school I volunteered to help clap chalk dust out of the erasers.

As I was gathering them up, Sister Angela said,

"Well, your parents must have been very pleased with your report card."

I sighed, my lips a thin line.

Sister's voice betrayed her surprise, "Not pleased?"

I shrugged. "My dad asked why I didn't have at least one A+."

"Oh, for crying out loud!" Sister said, her hands on her hips. "That's—" She clamped her mouth shut, probably before she said something rather unladylike, or perhaps I should say rather un-nunlike, if there is such a word.

"Is there any way I could get an A+?" I pleaded.

Now it was Sister who sighed. She considered it a moment, then asked, "What's your favorite subject?"

That was easy. "English!" You know how much I loved to read.

"I'll tell you what," she said. "You earn an A in English, and if you do a couple of extra book reports, I'll give you an A+."

A grin spread across my face.

I was going to earn that A+ and show it to my father, even if it killed me.

Which, in a way, it did.

16

You know, I have to give Scarlet credit for her inventive ways of coming after me. Every once in a while, I'd catch her looking at me during class, and her eyes would narrow as if to say *You just wait.*

One day in the hall she yanked my braid, then whispered in my ear, "I'm going to get you expelled!"

Okay, that was scary. I had no idea how she could accomplish such a feat, but I wouldn't put it past her to try.

Fortunately for me, that afternoon when I visited the church, Joshua was there. I hadn't seen him for weeks. Normally I would have been delighted, but Scarlet had me more than concerned.

Sitting in the back of the church, I poured out my frustration and anxiety to him.

"Don't you worry," he said. "God will arrange it so you will be okay."

I could only hope.

"Even God must find her difficult to deal with," I said.

Joshua just smiled. "Did you forgive her for tossing all those library books on the floor?"

"Yes. I forgave her by picking up the books myself." Wait. Had I told him what Scarlet had done? I guess I must have—otherwise how could he have known about it?

I stared him straight in the eye. "Are you going to disappear on me again?"

This produced a bigger smile. I'd never seen anybody smile with such joy as Joshua. "Oh, I'm always around. I'll be there when you need me the most."

Someone opened one of the church's side doors. Light spilled in from outside, and it was enough of a distraction to cause me to look away.

Yeah, when I looked back, I didn't see him anymore.

* * *

A few weeks later when I returned to the eighth-grade classroom after the lunch period, Sister Angela told us, "Boys and girls, I want all of you to stand next to your desks."

Frowning with puzzlement, I, along with the other students, stood. I glanced at Scarlet. She was smirking. Uh oh. She'd done something, but I had no idea what.

"The funds from the library are missing," Sister said. "All the boys will turn out their pockets."

That didn't take very long, and it produced only a few coins that could easily be explained away.

Afterward Sister said, "I want all of you to open the top of your desks and stand aside."

Our desks had lids that pulled upward to allow access to a storage space for pencils and books. Obediently, I raised mine . . . and wasn't the least bit surprised to see a couple of dollar bills and a pile of coins which hadn't been there before. So *that* was Scarlet's plan—to have me expelled for stealing from the school.

"Sister," I said calmly, "I think it's in my desk."

Sister Angela immediately stepped over to take a look. "Is this your money?" she asked me.

Before I had a chance to answer, Scarlet chimed in. "Sister, there's a way to tell. You remember right at the beginning of lunch I paid an overdue fine with a quarter. It was kind of funny-looking. It had some red stuff painted on it. I'm sure I could identify that coin."

Yeah, I bet she could identify that coin too. But you may be wondering why a quarter would have red on it. It's because, during the 1960 Presidential election, some people painted red nail polish on some quarters' image of George Washington to make him look like he was wearing the clothes of a Catholic cardinal. It was essentially saying a vote for a Catholic like Kennedy meant the pope would take over the United States. Several of these coins were still in circulation, although the nail polish was wearing off them.

Sister fingered the coins and picked up one with red on it. "This one?"

Scarlet nodded a little too enthusiastically. "That's the one! She must have taken the money. Everybody knows Markette spends all of lunchtime in the library."

"Anybody could have put that into my desk," I said.

"It had to be you," Scarlet insisted.

"Except," I said, "I couldn't have taken it. I wasn't in the library at lunch today."

"Sister," Scarlet said, "she's obviously lying!"

Full of confidence, I turned to Scarlet. What had

Joshua told me? *God will arrange it so you will be okay.*

Now, you know God works in mysterious ways. This time His mysterious way was breaking a toilet.

Yeah, you read that right. Breaking a toilet.

"But I have an alibi," I said. "Sister, you know how the upstairs toilet in the convent wasn't working right? And you called my father last night to have it repaired? Remember how he said he would send the part with me to school today? When the bell rang for lunchtime, I immediately went over to the convent. Sister Thomas let me in and I showed her how to fix it."

For a moment silence reigned in the classroom. Then Scarlet blurted, "That couldn't have taken the whole lunch period."

"It didn't," I replied. "Afterward, Sister Thomas took me into the convent kitchen and gave me some cookies and milk to thank me. We talked for a long time. Ask her. I was there until the bell rang. I think she was trying to talk me into becoming a nun."

At this, everybody stared at Scarlet, who was blushing a lovely shade of red. Not quite as red as the nail polish on the quarter, but red.

"Well, you said yourself anybody could have put that into your desk!"

"True," I said, scooping up the rest of the money and handing it to Suster Angela. "Anybody could have done it. Except me, of course."

I think it was obvious to everybody there I was forgiving Scarlet by letting her off the hook.

As we re-seated ourselves at our desks, I think

that, although it made her relieved, it also somehow made her more furious.

17

Graduation was only a month away. Mom took me shopping for an appropriate dress for the ceremony, which would be held the Saturday after the end of the school year. I picked out a pretty pastel blue one with a little bow at its empire waistline, but it cost $10! A whole $10! I'd never had any clothing so expensive. And it wasn't even from a thrift store.

To my utter surprise, Mom said she would pay it. I guess she figured a dress for such a significant occasion warranted the price. Maybe she wanted me dressed well in the photos she and Dad would undoubtedly mail to Great-uncle Mark.

As for me, I was thrilled—until I saw Scarlet wearing the exact same dress to church the next Sunday. For her it was just an everyday dress. Nothing special about it at all. I figured when I showed up wearing mine at graduation, she would make some kind of snide remark.

I didn't know it at the time, but I would not wear it to graduation.

This is the dress I would be buried in.

* * *

June 14, the final day of school, bloomed clear, sunny, and hot. At the kitchen table I ate my usual bowl of cereal, then dressed in jeans, a red shirt, and tennis shoes. I also donned my golden cross. After all, I had promised Great-uncle Mark I would wear it every day.

The last day was called Play Day, and the students not only had free dress instead of having to wear our uniforms, we got to spend the morning in the schoolyards. We girls were even allowed into the boys' yards this one day of the year.

At the door Mom said her usual goodbye. "Bye, bye, God bless, and be good. Look both ways before crossing the street, and don't step in any ink!"

I don't know why, but I gave her a peck on the cheek. "Thank you, Mommy."

"What was that for?" she asked, clearly surprised at the kiss and the fact that I had called her Mommy instead of Mom.

I wasn't quite sure myself. "I just wanted to."

Then I was off to school. I did not, of course, want to spend my day being bullied by Scarlet and company on the playground. I knew they would not miss any opportunity to get in their last licks. I opted to spend the morning in the school library.

The library was closed since nobody was going to be allowed to check out books, but I had told Sister Angela I would spend my time there straightening the shelves. She had gladly unlocked the door for me.

I grinned as I put the fiction section in order. I lovingly fingered the books that had transported me to the magical lands of Oz, Narnia, and Middle Earth. Oh, how I wished I could travel to some beautiful place like those.

After lunch, the entire student body, as usual, was herded into the parish hall to watch a movie. To my delight it was *Lilies of the Field*, the film I had been forbidden to watch at the drive-in all those years ago. Scarlet groaned when the title came up. For her this was old stuff, but for me it was brand new, and I was thrilled that I was finally going to get to watch it.

Then we were back in the eighth-grade room one more time to get our report cards.

Sister Angela winked when she handed me mine. There it was: all A's except for English. The A+!

When the bell rang, we cheered. Done with school for the year! Summer vacation, here we come!

I knew Dad didn't have a plumbing job that day, and I couldn't wait to show him my report card, so I left immediately instead of lingering a while so I wouldn't encounter Scarlet and her buddies on the walk home. If she did accost me, I knew it would be the last time.

I had no idea how right I was.

Standing at the corner of Main and Elm, I waited for the light to change while cars whizzed by. I was glancing at my report card and that lovely A+ when it was grabbed from behind.

I turned. Scarlet! "Oooo," she said. "Did you get some good grades?"

"Give that back!" I demanded.

Instead she glanced at it, then passed it to Verna who passed it to Damara. The light turned green, and we started across the street while they were playing keep-away with my report card.

"This isn't funny," I said, which only made them laugh.

We were almost to the other curb when Scarlet held the card up high, vertically, between her thumb and index finger, just out of my reach. I jumped, trying to grab it, but she was too tall.

"You want it?" She flung it into the air. "Go get it!"

It wheeled in the air a moment. Then a puff of wind blew it a few inches away.

No! My A+!

I figured I had plenty of time to get it. In the meantime, the other girls, laughing, stepped onto the opposite curb and continued down the street.

What I didn't know was that a woman driving a sports car was more interested in using her rear-view mirror to re-apply her lipstick than in watching the road.

She didn't see that her light was red.

I had just swept up my report card when everything seemed to slow to a crawl. I heard the roar of the car's engine but could not get my body to roll out of the way.

My last thought on Earth was wondering why a car had its headlights on during the day and why they were so blazingly bright.

Then I saw Joshua in the light, reaching out to me. He grasped both of my hands and took me, a split-second before impact.

18

Dying was easy, so much easier than I'd thought it would be.

Joshua and I, facing each other and still holding hands, hovered a few feet over the accident scene. I won't describe the gory details to you, but I will say I still had my report card clutched in my hand, and blood was seeping onto the golden cross Great-uncle Mark had given me so many years ago.

Scarlet, Verna, and Damara had turned around at the sound of screeching tires and a woman screaming.

It was all I looked at. I didn't care about the rest because now I saw for the first time that Joshua had been Jesus all along. And that was the way He looked now, grown up with a beard and mustache.

We communicated instantly with just our thoughts. My first one was a question, and I had only begun to think it when He gave me the answer. But I'll print those thoughts out in words for you. Every time you read about us "talking," it was really a mental exchange I've translated for you.

"How come you told me your name's Joshua? I know You don't lie."

"My name is Joshua. In Hebrew My name is Yeshua. The English translation of Yeshua is Joshua. So that is My name."

We smiled at each other, and He added, "I want to thank you for all the sandwiches."

"What? I didn't give you any . . . oh." Right.

Matthew 25:35. *For I was hungry, and you gave me to eat.*

Do you remember way back at the end of the prologue when I'd promised to tell you what it was like to encounter God after I died? I've held off getting to that because I thought you might first be wondering about the name Joshua.

But here goes . . .

This is not going to be easy to communicate to you. Words do not exist in any language that can give you the full impact. You'll excuse me if I occasionally use a metaphor in my attempts to explain.

Three things happened all at once, but I will describe them separately to make this easier for you.

The first was the overpowering Presence of God. He is everywhere, everywhere, everywhere! Yes, you know this already, but it is one thing to grasp this intellectually, another to experience it. All I can say is that He just IS. When Moses asked Him for His name, and He said "I Am Who Am," that is more right than I can tell you. He is like an arrow that points in only one direction, and it does not veer either to the right or to the left so much as the width of an atom. He is existence, reality, to the nth degree.

Second was an overwhelming peace flooding me. If you had asked me that morning to assign a number to the concept of peace, I would have given it a zero. In my mind peace had meant an absence of something, like war or belligerence.

This was nothing like that. This peace was palpable. Here I have to use a metaphor. Imagine it's a stormy night, but you've taken a hot bath, and you snuggle down into clean sheets. Despite the tempest raging around you, lightning flashing and thunder cracking, you feel completely safe.

Have you got the idea? Okay, now multiply that feeling by 1,000. Then you'll come close to getting the picture. If I had still been in my body, standing in a field with nuclear warheads exploding around me, mushroom clouds rising into the air, I still would have felt safe. That's how strong this peace is. It truly is a peace that surpasses understanding.

The third was God's Love. This is beyond all telling, but I'll try to tell you anyway. Again I have to use a metaphor. Imagine you've been baking something in a hot oven, but when you go to take it out, you forget to put on oven mitts and you scorch the tip of your finger. That's going to burn, and it's going to hurt.

Now imagine that when you scorch your finger it burns all right, but the sensation is pleasurable, and the pleasure is every bit as intense as the pain would normally be. That's what it would be like to feel this Love in your fingertip.

But of course I wasn't feeling it solely in my fingertip. It surged through all of me like hot lava. It was God's Love, it was my love for Him, all mixed together like two paints swirling to form a new, unique color. I realized I should have expected this. The Bible tells us God is Love, and that He is a Consuming Fire. That's His Nature. St. Peter says in his second epistle we become partakers of the Divine Nature, and boy! was I partaking! I was absolutely *burning* with Love for my Lord and Savior, Jesus Christ.

Oh! I just realized something.

If you're thinking of doing yourself in so you can experience all that, I have to tell you it won't work. You can't get closer to God by deliberately destroying the precious gift of life He's given you. No, that will not put you in His good Graces, and without being in His Grace, you will experience Fire, but I wouldn't count on it being pleasurable. Your death should be at the time of God's choosing. This ecstasy is for those faithful to Him. I can't say for certain where you would end up, but I wouldn't chance my eternal destiny. No, it's always best to accept God's Will in everything.

Below us the accident scene faded away, and, still holding hands, we zoomed through a tunnel of light, stopping in a place dense with fog.

"Where are we?" I asked. I wasn't the least bit disturbed by being in such a strange place. Jesus was with me, His burning Love still gushing through me.

"This is the Shekinah Glory Cloud," He told me.

Right. I'd studied about that in my religion class, about how the Old Testament said this had filled the temple of God. Check 2 Chronicles 5:14 if you want to see something about it.

Jesus said, "Here we will take a look at your life on Earth. I thought you would like some privacy for this."

And so began a full color, three-dimensional review of my short life.

19

Jesus showed me every bit of my life, all of it, from being conceived to the time of the accident. I saw my growth in the womb, my birth, and the discussion of my parents in the hospital afterward when they were trying to figure out how to name me after Dad's Uncle Mark.

To my surprise, not only were the scenes three-dimensional, I could perceive the thoughts and emotions of those who were there, what they were thinking and feeling.

And I do mean *everything* was there, including scenes that would normally cause embarrassment, like getting my diaper changed and going to the bathroom after I was potty trained. Yet none of it caused me the least bit of shame. It was simply the normal process of my body.

What did cause me shame were my sins. There were so many, especially ones I had brushed aside as minor and non-important. I couldn't believe how many lies I had told, and crossing my fingers behind my back obviously did nothing to turn a falsehood into the truth.

God couldn't pretend these sins weren't there. They were obviously there, in black and white, or perhaps I should say in living color. God's omniscient; therefore, of course He knew all about them.

So, despite the wonderful Love surging through me, I experienced every bit of the pain I had deliberately caused, which, when you think about it, is only fair. Several of these sins weren't actions I'd done but actions I didn't do. For example, often when Mom had called me to set the table for dinner, I had pouted, grumbling about having my precious reading time interrupted. Mom had always thanked me afterward for helping, but I saw, and experienced, how badly it disappointed her that I never thanked her for the work she'd done preparing the meal. Even though I knew I should have, I couldn't be bothered to thank her, not once! This was hardly honoring my mother and father as we are commanded to do.

I saw the scene in the Hansen's living room when Scarlet had punched me in the nose. To my surprise, later on in my life, she had been telling the truth when she'd said Linda hadn't wanted me to have her new address.

I saw too why she had broken my nose. But I understand Scarlet wants to tell you the reason herself, so I'm afraid you're going to have to wait a while longer for the explanation.

Oh, c'mon. You can stand it. Patience is a virtue.

Even my thoughts were there, like my daydream at the drive-in when I mentally squished Scarlet with an aircraft carrier. That was far less than nice. Oh, and praying to have different parents or plead to go live with Great-uncle Mark instead? What horrible things to pray for! Again, I wasn't honoring my father and my mother.

I could have, I saw, used the time stuck in the backseat for a far better purpose, like praying for something good. Instead, I had wasted it on a ridiculous princess fantasy.

This suffering I was undergoing was God's way of applying Christ's merits to purge my imperfections, and I noticed the pain from these sins wasn't as severe if I had repented. And you know that verse in the Bible "Blessed are the merciful: for they shall obtain mercy"? So true! Forgiving others played a *huge* part in this—Christ was forgiving my trespasses as I had forgiven those who had trespassed against me. I also noticed that as Jesus obliterated my sins, it left more space in my soul for His fiery Love.

This sounds like I'm making the Life Review all bad. Oh, it wasn't! The good I did was there as well: like giving my lunch to the bum on Main Street. I experienced the quelling of his horrible hunger as he wolfed down that first bologna sandwich. I had his delight at later finding the Hershey bar at the bottom of the paper sack—he hadn't had chocolate for years.

You know how you've been told to do unto others as you would have them do unto you? Well, guess what. What you do unto others is done unto you in your Life Review. It's right there in the Bible: Luke 6:38. All good reasons to not only repent of certain things but to get out there and create some joy!

I can't tell you how long the Review lasted. Time is different in eternity. It could have been years. It could have been a moment. To God one day is as a thousand years, and a thousand years is as one day. Eternity touches all chronological time.

I know this is a difficult concept to grasp when you're still in the world. Think of it this way: if the biography of your life was contained in a book, well, from outside the book all the time of your life is there, past and future. No matter what page you'd flip to, that would, at the moment, be the present.

At the end of the Life Review, Jesus clasped my hands again. "Thou art all fair, O my love, and there is not a spot in thee. Behold, I make all things new!" Yes, He was quoting scripture, Song of Solomon 4:7 and Revelation 21:5, but now I saw these verses in a new light. He had made me perfect, ready for the perfection of Heaven.

This was my real self, my true self. This was what God always had intended for me to be.

The gray fog surrounding us dissipated into a beautiful garden radiating with colors I had never seen before. You know how in your age there are special glasses for the colorblind which enable them to see the regular colors of the world? This was like getting a super-endowed pair of those.

Jesus had that lovely smile of His. "I have a surprise for you."

And boy, did I get a surprise!

Linda! Linda was there!

We hugged and she showed me a scene from when she was ten years old.

* * *

The grocery store was crowded on Saturday, big band music playing through the store speakers as shoppers scurried about, filling their carts.

I hope we get Cheerios, Linda thought, trailing

her mother in the grocery store. *I really like Cheerios.*

"Mom, can we get some Cheerios?" she asked.

Mom drew her straight brunette hair behind her ear and sighed. "Honey, no. We're just going to pick up a few things to take with us on the road."

That was true. Barely anything was in their cart. Toothbrushes, toothpaste. Bandages. A couple of boxes of cookies and two more of crackers.

Mom rounded the corner of an aisle and crashed into another cart. "Oh! Evelyn! So sorry!"

There was Mrs. Hansen with her daughter Scarlet. "No harm done," Mrs. Hansen remarked.

"Hi, Scarlet," Linda said.

"Hi," Scarlet echoed with almost no feeling.

"Getting ready for the new school year?" Mrs. Hansen asked.

"Um . . . no. In fact, Linda will not be returning."

At this Scarlet's head perked up.

"No?" Mrs. Hansen asked.

"No. We're moving to Memphis."

"Whoa, that's quite a distance. Why Memphis? Did your husband get a new job?"

"No . . . um, it's where St. Jude's Hospital is, you know, the one Danny Thomas founded?"

Mrs. Hansen's eyes shot wide. "Oh! Do you mean that . . . "

Linda's mother merely nodded.

Mrs. Hansen glanced at Linda. "Oh, I'm so sorry to hear that." She opened her purse and pulled out a paper and pencil. "Here. Let me give you my address and phone number. You call me anytime you need to talk, day or night."

"And let me give you mine," Linda's mother said. "My husband has already put down the deposit on an apartment there."

They scribbled for a while, then exchanged papers. Linda pulled Scarlet aside. "Don't give my new address to Markette. Please!"

Mom and Dad thought she didn't know why they had to move. They thought she didn't understand how sick she was, what the word *leukemia* meant.

But she had seen the fear in their eyes.

Markette should not have to go through knowing about that. No, it would hurt her too much.

It was better if she left without saying a word to any of her classmates.

Scarlet shrugged. "I won't give her your address. I promise."

* * *

Remember I told you way back in the beginning that there was a child who bravely faced the end of her life? Yeah, that was Linda.

But now we could be together with nothing to separate us ever again.

And we would be together in the most magnificent land of all.

20

Jesus asked me, "Would you like to attend your funeral?"

I could tell by the way He said it that He thought this would be a good idea. So of course I said yes, and the next thing I knew, I was there.

I don't know how many days this took place after my death, and I didn't care. Time no longer had any real meaning to me.

I entered the church from the back, sliding right through the heavy door I'd opened the day I'd met Joshua. There was the cry room where I'd been sobbing about all my troubles. There were the pews in the back, now empty, where Joshua and I'd had our conversations. I smiled as I realized I'd been talking to Jesus all that time.

Organ music softly played. My casket was at the front, closed, although I could see my body inside. Yes, I did get to wear the blue dress I had picked out. Looped around my neck was the golden cross and necklace Great-uncle Mark had given me.

A huge bouquet of white lilies was on top of my casket. An abundance of other flowers—roses, carnations, and more lilies—were stacked in front of the altar. I figured they were all probably from Great-uncle Mark.

He, Mom, and Dad were in one of the front pews, sitting stoically, although once in a while a tear dripped from Mom's eye. Great-uncle Mark was choking with sobs.

I floated up to Dad and placed my hand on his. "It's all right, Daddy. I'm okay."

Mom I kissed on the forehead. She must have felt a little bit of something because she brushed her palm over her skin. "I love you, Mommy."

Great-uncle Mark I hugged. I could hear his thoughts. *I should have made more of an effort to visit. No! I had to let work get in the way. I thought I had plenty of time, but now this! How am I supposed to ever get over this?*

"Trust in Jesus and you will be all right. I love you, Great-uncle Mark."

Scarlet and her parents entered the nave. Scarlet's knees buckled at the sight of the casket, and her parents practically had to pick her up off the floor.

One of my female cousins whispered, "She must have loved her very much."

The three of them scooted into a pew, Scarlet sandwiched between her folks. Her eyes, I saw, were hollow, expressionless. Numb, she glanced at her lap and started cleaning her fingernails.

Mrs. Hansen passed Scarlet a memorial pamphlet that had a smiling picture of me with my full name, Markette Maria Mason, and my dates of birth and death: January 22, 1954—June 14, 1968. Scarlet glanced at it, then set it aside.

Verna and Damara slid into the pew behind her.

"Scarlet?" Damara whispered. "You okay?"

A shake of her head was barely perceptible.

Mrs. Hansen turned around. "You girls should be with your parents."

Obligingly they crossed the aisle to sit on the other side of the church.

I stared at Scarlet, reading her mind. Two scenes kept repeating over and over in her brain. *Why don't you do the world a favor? Why don't you just drop dead?* and, flinging my report card into the air, *You want it? Go get it!*

"I forgive you," I said. I knew she couldn't hear me, but maybe she'd sense a bit of the message like Mom had gotten a bit of the kiss. "I forgive you for all of it."

No reaction. She just sat, fussing with her nails.

Then I was back in Heaven.

* * *

Jesus was there, waiting for me.

"I'm concerned about Scarlet," I said. "She's not dealing with this well. In fact, she's not dealing with it at all."

"Do you remember how I told you," Jesus said, "that good can come out of evil?"

"Yes."

"Well, a lot of good can come out of this. And," He added, "you can help."

Part II

Scarlet

Consider the lilies, how they grow: they labour not, neither do they spin. But I say to you, not even Solomon in all his glory was clothed like one of these.

Luke 12:27

If your sins be as scarlet, they shall be made as white as snow.

Isaiah 1:18

21

My name is Scarlet Ann Hansen, and I died when I was fifty-one years old.

I was murdered.

My death made the national news, in most places the top story. Not that I cared. I was already dead.

Markette has already told you about the events that led to her death, how they were like dominos tipping over, one after the other.

The first domino that eventually led to my death occurred the very same day we five-year-old girls, Markette, Verna, and I, were playing with our dolls one hot summer afternoon at my house.

The two of them were discussing nursing their apparently deathly ill dolls back to health. I bragged that since my daddy was a doctor, my baby never got sick.

That's about the time I felt nature call and announced, "I need to pee."

Off I toddled past the kitchen where our mothers were playing cards and gossiping. I did my business in the bathroom, then headed back through the hallway.

That's when I heard my mother say something I wish she had never uttered. Or that I had never heard. Who knows how differently everything would have turned out if only she'd said something else? Not that I'm blaming her, mind you. I'm the one who chose to act upon what she said.

"Wouldn't you know Scarlet had to inherit that awful hook nose my father had," Mommy said in an off-hand casual remark. "I wish she'd gotten a cute little button nose like Markette did."

I stopped, stunned. Something was wrong with my nose?

I scrambled back to the bathroom, peered into the mirror, and touched the bridge with my finger. Okay, there was a bump in the middle, a rather prominent bump at that. I later learned this is called an aquiline nose. The tip did kind of veer over a bit in a hook. If you think of Margaret Hamilton as the Wicked Witch of the West in the movie version of *The Wizard of Oz*, you'll kind of get the idea.

Soreness ringed my throat. This goes to show you how parents should be more careful what they say when their children could be listening.

I stomped into the living room. There was Markette, turning her plastic baby bottle upside down and righting it again, over and over.

Standing before her, I gazed at her cute little button nose.

My eyes narrowed; my lips stiffened. It wasn't fair! How come she got a terrific nose and I didn't? I just plain couldn't stand it! I'd show her!

I drew my fist back and punched her nose as hard as the rage in my five-year-old arm could manage. Something crunched and blood spurt.

Honestly, I didn't want to hurt her. My child brain didn't think that far ahead.

Markette immediately started howling.

Uh oh. I realized only then that I hadn't thought

this through. The ruckus brought all the ladies dashing into the room.

"What did you do?" Mrs. Mason asked, kneeling before Markette. Wow, she was already assuming Markette was responsible.

Markette pointed. "She hit me!"

Uh oh again. Boy, would I get into trouble for this. I couldn't envision how bad the spanking was going to be.

Mommy demanded, "Scarlet, did you hit Markette?"

That's when I realized I could get away with this by lying. After all, even Markette's mother supposed it was her own fault. I opened my eyes as wide as possible, as if I couldn't believe the accusation, and said, "No, Mommy."

"She did too!" Markette insisted.

Meanwhile, a small bundle of ice in a washcloth arrived, and Mrs. Mason applied it to Markette's nose. The ladies then turned their attention to Verna, who had observed the whole incident.

"Verna?" my neighbor's mommy asked. "Did Scarlet hit Markette?"

Uh oh again! I had forgotten there was a witness!

I did the only thing I could do, if I wanted to get away with it. Staring at Verna, I narrowed my eyes, tightened my lips, and clenched my hand. She got the message, all right.

I counted myself incredibly lucky the ladies had their attention focused on Verna instead of me.

Verna gulped. And caved. "No."

"Then how," Verna's mother asked, "did she get hurt?"

"Um . . . she fell down."

"That's right!" I blurted, utterly relieved that Verna had come up with a reason for the bloody nose. "She fell down!"

I admit I felt bad about Markette being yanked to her feet and repeatedly spanked by her mother.

But I didn't feel bad enough about it to tell the truth and get spanked instead.

* * *

The next time Markette's mother brought her to our house, I couldn't help pointing and laughing at her crooked nose.

"Scarlet!" Mommy scolded. "We do not treat our guests like that! You will apologize immediately!"

I'd learned from the previous incident what the word *apologize* meant. "Sorry," I said.

I was not sorry.

"Now, you girls be nice," Mommy said. "Scarlet has a new game she wants to play with you."

I'd gotten Candy Land a few weeks before and was already tired of it. I began, "But I didn't say I wanted—"

Mommy's glare cut me off.

"Okay, let's play."

Now, this may sound strange to you, but I was ticked at Markette. I had to prove to myself, and especially to her, that I was better. I had to justify breaking her nose, so my brain told me she deserved it . . . and anything else I did to her.

The moment our mothers' backs were turned, I yanked her braid.

"Ow!"

"Is something wrong?" Mrs. Mason asked.

I gave Markette an intimidating glare.

"No," she said.

But here was another problem. When I'd touched her hair, I had been amazed at how soft and silky it was, even in a braid. My hair, on the other hand, was a frizzy red with a texture more like straw. The teenage boy who lived next door had laughingly compared it to the hair of Bozo the Clown. Honestly, it didn't look *that* bad, but his nasty comment still stung.

While our mothers had coffee in the living room, I brought Candy Land to the kitchen table, opened it, and spread out the board. After a quick explanation of the rules, I grabbed a plastic gingerbread man as my playing piece. I was determined to make Markette believe my hair was better than hers.

"I always play with the red one," I said. "It's a pretty color, like my ponytail. And everybody knows ponytails are better than braids like yours, especially brown ones." I then told her that her hair was the color of what comes out of people's butts.

I admit the word I used wasn't a very nice one.

Her eyes filled with pain. But I wasn't done.

"No wonder your daddy's a plumber who works with toilets."

Of course I could not allow Markette to win the game. This involved a little cheating on my part.

Okay, a lot of cheating. And I was going to win, thereby proving my superiority . . . until Markette drew the card for the Ice Cream Floats, which advanced her close to the end.

My jaw dropped. "That's not fair!"

"But that's the rules," she said, scooting her blue piece along the path to the proper square.

No. I could not lose. Losing was bad enough, but losing to her? In my anger I upset the board, cards and game pieces clattering over the table and floor. There! That would keep her from winning!

It made enough noise to draw our mothers from the living room. "What is going on in here?" Mommy asked.

Uh oh. I was about to get into trouble, unless . . .

I pointed at Markette. "She cheats! And she didn't like that I was winning, so she threw everything on the table!"

Markette's jaw dropped. Her mother yanked her out of her chair and spanked her precious little behind. Then she was dragged into the living room. I couldn't hear what she and her mother were saying in there, but I knew it couldn't be good for Markette.

After a while, she returned to the kitchen. "I'm sorry."

Wow. This was great! Not only had I avoided a spanking but Markette had gotten it instead and been forced to apologize for what I'd done.

Surely that showed her who had the power here.

Claiming and blaming. Claiming innocence and blaming someone else. Just like I'd done when I'd

punched Markette in the nose.
　　I was winning this game.
　　Okay, I was cheating, but I was still winning.

22

The first day of first grade, as I was standing before the bathroom mirror, I asked Mommy, "Would you please put my hair into a braid instead of a ponytail?" Despite what I had told Markette, I thought her braid was really pretty.

Mommy stood behind me. "That is not a good idea," she said, tugging a comb through my red locks.

"But Markette gets a braid every day," I pouted.

"You," Mommy said, "are not Markette. Your hair is different. It's frizzy, and braiding it can make it even frizzier." She poured some yellowish ointment onto her hands and smoothed it over my hair. I hated the ointment. It had a funny smell and made my hair look oily.

Mommy combed the stuff all through my hair, then swept it up into a ponytail. She clipped in a big white bow just above the rubber band.

"There! Don't you look pretty!"

I gazed at myself in the mirror. Still the same stupid bump on my nose. Still the same bright red frizzy hair all glossy with ointment. At least the blue plaid uniform looked nice.

The doorbell rang. "That should be your friends," Mommy said. Sure enough, when she opened the front door, there stood Verna and a new girl from down the block, Damara.

Mommy handed me my Flintstones lunch box and gave me a kiss on the forehead. Then we three headed off for our first day.

After a few blocks of giggling and comparing the cartoon pictures on our lunchboxes, we came to the corner of Main and Elm. And guess who we came up behind as she was waiting for the signal to change. That brown braid was easy to recognize.

I yanked it hard. "Well, if it isn't Crook Nose!"

Markette turned around.

"Wow," Damara said. "That is the ugliest nose I've ever seen."

"Probably the ugliest nose in the world," I added.

We laughed. I shoulder-shoved Markette aside when the light turned green. She almost fell, which I found even more amusing.

As my two friends and I continued down the next block a few yards ahead of Markette, I devised what I thought was a wonderful idea. "Let's pretend we're talking about her," I whispered. I cupped my hands over Verna's ear like I was telling her something. She in turn did the same with Damara. Then we glanced back at Markette and snickered.

The distress in her eyes was enough to keep us going with the ruse until we arrived at school.

Frankly, I was delighted by the incident. Coming up with the idea of this little prank established me as the leader of our group. Besides, now I wasn't the only one picking on Markette.

Somehow that validated the teasing in my six-year-old mind. After all, if they were doing it too, it must be okay, right?

And it was the three of us against the one of her.

I liked those odds.

And so it was . . . until we stepped into the classroom.

After a few moments, Markette squealed, "Linda!"

She and this other brown-haired girl hugged, bouncing up and down on their toes.

Oh, great. She had a friend. And a good friend, from the looks of it.

If I did something to Markette but pleaded innocence, Verna and Damara were sure to back me up, and it would be the word of three against one. But Linda would also be a witness, which complicated things . . .

. . . if this friend would stand up for her.

At recess while we were waiting in line for the slide, I tested that by trying to tug the braid again. Linda, fire blazing in her eyes, stomped her foot and stepped between us. "Markette is my friend!" she declared. "You leave her alone!"

Rats.

* * *

That afternoon we had reading time. I sighed. I hated reading. It was so hard, essentially trying to break a code. So many words weren't pronounced the way they were spelled, which, when you think about it, is incredibly stupid. Why did adults have to make things so complicated for kids?

Sister Rose started the lesson by having us flip to a word list in the back of our textbooks. She had the class say each word aloud, then she explained what they meant. I glanced at Markette. She was slumped in her seat, fingers softly tapping her desktop. I realized she wasn't happy about this either but for a different reason.

She was bored and waiting impatiently to get to the story.

Wouldn't you know Sister had us read out loud. Each student took a turn, one paragraph each. When my turn came, I gripped the sides of my book and gritted my teeth.

We'd been taught some reading in kindergarten, but this was tougher. With almost every word Sister had to tell me, "Sound it out." Then I came to the word *between*, which I read as "bet-ween." After all, wasn't I supposed to split a word into syllables between the consonants? I got corrected on that one too.

I let out my breath when I arrived at the end of the paragraph. Whew!

A few students later, it was Markette's turn.

Oh, my goodness. She breezed through the first sentence so quickly Sister cried, "Markette! Slow down! The other boys and girls can't keep up!"

She slowed a bit but Sister had to admonish her again that she was still going too fast.

That's when Markette began reading one. word. at. a. time. She wasn't fumbling with pronunciations like I had been, but I thought she was mocking me, especially when the other kids laughed at how funny it sounded. I took it as a deliberate smack in my face. I understand now she was only trying to obey Sister. It wasn't a personal attack, but at the time it sure seemed like one.

Inwardly, I seethed. I figured she could read almost as well as a grown-up.

You have no idea what it was like to be forced to sit day after day in the same room with this girl who was prettier and smarter than me, who always had that gorgeous braid of silky hair. Every time we got work back from Sister Rose, I surreptitiously glanced at her grades, and they were always better than mine, sometimes way better.

My dislike of Markette was blooming into a full-blown hatred.

I believe it was G.K. Chesterton who said something about it being impossible to stay on one level of evil. That road, he'd said, goes down and down.

And I was turning into the perfect example of that.

23

One afternoon on the way home from school, I gave Markette an insult I would later come to regret. "Why don't you do the world a favor?" I asked over my shoulder as I, Verna, and Damara were crossing at the intersection of Main and Elm, snickering. "Why don't you just drop dead?"

Honestly, I didn't mean it, but years later, she did drop dead. Right there at that intersection.

And right at the place where she happened to be standing when I said it.

* * *

One of the most difficult parts of school for me was report cards. When I brought home my first one from second grade, I figured I had done well. I had turned in all my homework. I had passed all my tests. I hadn't passed them as well as Markette, of course, but still . . . these were good grades, right?

I happily showed it to Mommy in the living room. My smile evaporated when she frowned.

"A C+ in English?" she said.

Hey, c'mon! Reading is hard! She signed the card, and I didn't think very much of it until the next day after school when I walked into the kitchen.

I got myself some cookies and milk. Mom was at the table, reading a magazine. She looked up and casually said, "Did you know Markette got an A in English? I'm surprised the daughter of a doctor couldn't manage at least a B."

Obviously our two mothers had had a visit or a

phone conversation. This was all I needed, being told by my own mom that I didn't measure up to Markette. I mean, I already knew that, but I didn't want my parents, of all people, to know it.

Even though the cookies were chocolate chip, my favorite, they were pretty tasteless.

* * *

And so a few school years passed. Every day I was forced to sit in the same room with this girl who, just by being there, was a constant reminder that she was better than me in every way, a girl who was everything I desperately wanted to be.

But wasn't.

Each and every report card was compared to Markette's . . . and found wanting. Sometimes it was even test scores or grades on book reports.

In my mind the high scores came naturally to Markette the same way her silky hair came naturally. I had to study like crazy to get the grades I did, but she seemed to breeze through everything. I never saw her studying, so I figured she didn't have to.

Grrrrrr!

It was like having my deficiencies continuously shoved in my face. Honestly, how was that supposed to make me feel?

I realize now more was going on than I knew at the time. My mother had scored by marrying a doctor, a prominent surgeon. We lived in an expensive two-story house with a pool. Mrs. Mason was stuck with a plumber and lived in the poorer section of town. In order to compensate for the divergence in their social status, Mrs. Mason bragged about how well Markette did in school. It was the one thing she had better than her former schoolmate, my mother.

Knowing my mother, I am sure she was not the least bit pleased with coming up short in this department.

Life, she was teaching me, was a competition.

It was a lesson I was learning all too well.

Competition over social status was the reason I flouted mine to Markette at every opportunity. I was very happy to point out that we had a huge house with a pool, and she didn't. I got to wear pretty bows in my hair while she was stuck with just a simple rubber band and what I called her "ugly braid."

So, when she showed up at the drive-in wearing what had to be the world's ugliest cow pajamas and was essentially forced to the playground in them, I was delighted.

I couldn't wait to get to school that Monday with the news about those—and having everybody mooing at her during recess.

Yeah, I knew it hurt her. I *wanted* it to hurt her.

I didn't stop to think about what kind of person I was rapidly becoming: someone who took joy in causing another's misery.

Of course, Linda put a stop to it.

If only I could get rid of Linda.

* * *

Then I got lucky. The summer after fourth grade, Linda got rid of herself.

Mom and I ran into Linda and her mother in the grocery store, and that's when I heard she was moving really far away! I understand you've already been told the story about what happened in the supermarket, so I won't repeat it here.

But I was delighted to let Markette know the first day of fifth grade that Linda was gone for good. At the beginning of recess, I was dribbling a basketball and showing off my prowess with it in front of the other girls. Dad had set up a hoop in our backyard, and I had practiced plenty just for this purpose.

That's when Markette wondered, aloud, where Linda was.

Delighted that she had brought up the subject, I grabbed the ball between my hands. "Linda's not coming back," I said smugly. "She moved away." Of course I had to add an insult. "She probably got tired of looking at your ugly crooked nose."

As if that was actually the reason she'd moved. Yeah, like her parents had packed up all their belongings and moved cross-country to get away from someone's nose. I was sure nobody believed that, but it was another opportunity to point out how awful Markette's nose looked and I wasn't about to pass up the chance.

I bounced the basketball twice, enjoying Markette's wide-eyed distress. "I have her new address," I bragged.

"Well, may I have it?" Markette asked.

I took one deliberate step toward her, moving in for the kill. "She said not to give it to you."

This was telling all the other girls *Do you see? Linda chose me! She chose me over Markette! Even she knows I'm better than her!*

Oh, yeah. Markette's lower lip trembling told me she had gotten that message too.

* * *

You already read what happened at my thirteenth birthday party, so I won't say much about it except to fill in some details you may not know.

Over a week before the party, Mom handed me the envelopes that contained the invitations.

"Be sure to mail these on your way to school," she said. "You can hand Verna and Damara the ones for them."

Except for those two, the others had 5¢ first class stamps on them. I was happy to give my two best friends their invites when they arrived at our door that morning for our usual walk together to school. When we reached the mailbox at the corner of Main and Elm, though, I sorted through the rest. They were for other girls from school and some family members, like a female cousin my age.

Of course there was one for Markette. As the daughter of my mother's best friend, she was naturally on the guest list.

Grinning, I showed this invitation to Verna and Damara. "What should I do with this one?"

Laughing, we came up with some suggestions I won't mention except to say they weren't very sanitary.

We settled on ripping it into little pieces and tossing them into the air like confetti.

24

I had never been so horribly steamed at Markette as I was at that party. First, she showed up, uninvited . . . at least uninvited by me. Then she handed me a gift meant for little kids, not the grown-up teen I considered myself.

It didn't hit me until years later that her mom had probably been in a big fat hurry at the toy store and grabbed the first thing she saw. And of course my destruction of Markette's invitation was the reason she was rushing. So, to my shame, I am responsible for that lousy gift.

At the time, though, I hadn't figured this out, and I held Markette responsible, especially for the hot embarrassment burning my cheeks when I had to apologize to *her,* of all people, in front of my friends and classmates. Oh, and for me getting grounded. After all, I didn't want to blame myself for that, and *Mark*ette was, well, such an easy *mark* to vent my rage upon.

That night in bed I stared at the dark ceiling and thought about how I would exact my revenge. *Maybe I could bribe some other students to pick on her,* I thought. *Yeah, especially the boys. A few of the boys in the younger grades think girls are yucky, so they might be willing to walk up to her and tell her how stupid and ugly she is. Five cents apiece should do it.*

I stuck five nickels into my lunch sack Monday morning, ready to experiment how well that would work.

Then, on the way to school, Verna, Damara, and I, amid the normal whoosh of cars zooming past, happened to stroll up the sidewalk behind Markette stopped by a red light at the corner of Main and Elm.

"Hey, Crook Nose!" I sneered.

She turned around and stated plainly, "Are you talking to me?"

I was so shocked I couldn't speak. Her nose was fixed!

But there was more. As the cross traffic whizzed by, her face had a serenity she'd never displayed before, reflecting an inward beauty beyond anything earthly. It almost seemed like she was . . . dare I say it? *Glowing.*

I stood there, agape. Obviously, something had happened, something amazing, but for the life of me I couldn't figure out what.

I'm sure I looked like an idiot, standing there with my eyes and mouth both open wide.

The signal turned green and Markette started across the street. The three of us were frozen, too thunderstruck to move.

She turned around, saw us still standing on the curb. "Aren't you coming?"

We walked several paces behind her all the way to school, occasionally glancing at each other as if to ask *What happened?*

* * *

During math that morning, my brain kept trying to process this new development. Once in a while, I glanced at Markette, who sat two rows over from me.

Sister Ursula, our seventh-grade teacher, stood at the blackboard. "Scarlet!" she admonished. "I asked you to solve this equation! If $2x + 9 = 3x + 6$, what is x?"

"Um . . . um . . ." Math was my best subject, but I was so distracted my mental faculties had flown out the window. X? 9? 3? 6? All the constants and variables seemed to jumble into one incomprehensible puzzle.

Hands of other students shot up. "Markette?" Sister asked.

"X equals three," she answered.

She would have to be the one to show me up. And, even worse, I saw that Tony, the blond, blue-eyed boy I had a secret crush on, had turned in his seat in front of Markette to gaze at her. His sloppy grin spanned from ear to ear, and he had a new twinkle in his eyes. Oh, great. Not only had Markette stolen my thunder, she was stealing the boy I liked too!

* * *

Damara had a book due at the school library, so during recess she, Verna, and I headed over there. The place was empty—well, at least I thought it was empty—except for the musty smell of hundreds of books. Sister Thomas was supposed to be manning the circulation desk, but apparently she had once again forgotten to show up.

"What do you suppose happened?" Damara asked, placing her book on the desk. She didn't have to say what subject she was talking about. The whole school was buzzing with the news about Markette's nose.

"Well, she must have seen a doctor," Verna answered. "Maybe that's why she left the party early, because she had a doctor's appointment."

"I can't believe this," I snarled. "Already she was the prettiest girl in school, and look at her now!"

"You can tell she's going to be really beautiful when she grows up," Verna added.

That was obvious. Before, the first thing anyone had noticed about Markette had been the mess of a nose in the middle of her face. It was such a distinctive defect that it was difficult to gaze at anything else. Since now her "cute little button nose" was back, attention was drawn to her big brown eyes with their long dark lashes. I figured by the time she was in high school no boy would be able to resist her.

"This is so unfair!" I growled. "She's pretty, she's smart, and you know what else? You ever hear of Mark Mason?"

"The gazillionaire?" Damara asked. "The one who plays golf with President Johnson?"

"Yeah," I said. "Him. My mom told me Markette's related to him. She was even named after him! He's the one who pays for her tuition here."

"Really?" Verna and Damara gasped in unison.

"Her dad is his only relative, so guess who's getting all that money when he dies. And guess who will get it later when her dad dies."

"Oh, my gosh," Damara said. "Markette's going to be filthy rich?"

I clenched my fists. "I hate her. I hate her so much. She gets it all. She gets looks, and smarts, and money. And she hasn't done anything to deserve any of it."

The bell ending recess trilled.

We headed to class, my problem unresolved.

* * *

Amid all the screeching and hollering of younger students as we spilled out of the school's side door and headed for the playground at lunchtime, I realized my plan to bribe others to pick on Markette didn't seem like such a hot option now. Not only that, but to my dismay when I got to the lunch tables, many other girls in the class had gathered around her to check out the new shape of her nose, complimenting her on how nice it looked. Even a few of the boys, who had come into the yard to use the drinking fountain, wanted to examine it, including beautiful blue-eyed Tony. Wouldn't you know he was practically flirting with her!

The moment he was out of hearing range, I sauntered up behind Markette and said, "Hey, stupid! Your nose may be better, but you're still ugly!"

She turned around. "So . . . you're superior to me?"

My eyes widened. Wait. What was this? And why was she so calm?

"You bet I am!" I said. Well, what else could I say?

"And I'm inferior to you."

"That's right!"

"And it's obvious to everybody? Really, really obvious?"

I smirked. "It sure is! Even more obvious than your stupid nose!"

Okay, I should have realized she was up to something, but I was so delighted with her statements that I couldn't help agreeing.

Hey, what else was I supposed to do? Disagree with what she was saying?

"Well," Markette said, facing the other girls, "she must think you're incredibly stupid. It's obvious she's superior and I'm inferior, but she has to keep proving it to you over and over and over again. Or . . . maybe, just maybe, she doesn't really think she's such hot stuff but wants you to believe it."

Iona tittered. A few of the others followed suit. Warmth flooded my cheeks as the titters evolved into giggles.

"That's not true!" I shrieked, realizing only as I said it that my tone of voice betrayed just how true it was.

"Isn't it?" she asked, stepping toward me. "If it isn't, why is your face turning red?"

Not knowing what else to do, I stomped away.

But I was determined to find a way to get back at her.

Already, as I ate my lunch, the gears in my brain were spinning.

25

By the next day I had come up with a plan. It wasn't easy because calling Markette names was no longer going to work. But, to my shame, I have to admit I could be quite the evil genius if I wanted to be. And, to my shame, I have to admit I was incredibly good at dragging others down into iniquity with me.

On the way to school that bright sunny day I told Verna and Damara about my scheme.

Damara bit her lip. She was obviously the weakest link. "I don't know. We could really get into trouble."

"Not if we stick together," I pointed out. "It's three against one."

She said, "But the other girls . . ."

"Will say nothing. I'll let it be known during recess what I think of tattlers. And that the same thing could happen to tattlers who tattle."

"Okay. I guess."

"Pinkie swear," I insisted at the corner of Main and Elm. While waiting for the signal to change, we wrapped our right little fingers around each other's, although Damara did so a bit reluctantly. This sealed the deal. We considered pinkie swears inviolate, and none of us would dare break such a solemn oath.

That afternoon, however, before I could put my plan into action, Markette announced, "I have something to say in front of everyone."

My eyes narrowed. *Now* what was Markette up to? Was she going to humiliate me again?

The girls gathered around her, and Markette sucked in a deep breath. "I want to apologize to Scarlet for what I said yesterday. It wasn't right, and I'm sorry."

Well, what do you know! The idiot was actually making this easier for me!

I took three deliberate steps toward her. "I do *not* accept your apology," I said and immediately put my plan into action. I grabbed her sack lunch and tossed it to Verna, who tossed it to Damara.

It was the last thing Markette expected. We began a game of keep-away, which wasn't hard since Markette was so darn short. After making her run ragged trying to get her lunch back, I tossed it over my head and into the school dumpster. All that basketball practice had turned out to be beneficial in a way I had never anticipated.

"Oops," I said sarcastically and walked away.

* * *

You already know what happened. I got away with it! Yup, claiming innocence and blaming Markette really worked!

Well, I should say I got away with it in this world. I experienced all the daily hunger I had inflicted on Markette in my Life Review after I died.

But that was later.

One afternoon Markette didn't show up at the lunch tables. "Do you know where she is?" I asked my comrades in crime.

Verna shrugged.

Damara said, "Maybe she got sick and went home."

Nope. Markette was in class for the afternoon session. I blinked in surprise, then frowned. Where had she disappeared to?

Several lunchtimes later, I found her in the library. This was a bit of a surprise because I knew no eating was allowed in there. But Markette smiled and winked at me. Yeah, she knew full well I couldn't do a thing to her there, not with Sister Angela at the front desk.

Well, phooey!

I didn't have much chance with Markette until summer vacation rolled around and our moms insisted on throwing us together, usually at our pool. To my surprise, this time Markette took all the teasing and the splashing in her face in stride.

I wondered more and more what was going on with her. Maybe she was just maturing? If she was, she was doing it much faster than I was.

Which only infuriated me more.

But that was nothing compared to the simmering rage building inside me the day after we got our eighth-grade midterm report cards.

I'd scored all A's with one A- in English. Surely I'd beaten Markette this time . . . or at least duplicated her, right?

Wrong!

In the kitchen I nearly choked on my after-school snack of cookies and milk when Mom said, "Markette got straight A's." Her shoulders slumped. "Well, I guess you did the best you could."

Hey! Excuse me! That was a damn good report card! I'd knocked myself out getting those grades! And here I was being told it was only "the best you could"? Like I was so inferior, that was all I could manage?

Okay, fine. Next time I'd bring the A- up to an A.

Let's see Markette beat that!

* * *

A few years before I'd gotten this weird quarter in change at a store. It had some red on it, and I'd asked Mom about it, but she'd said she had no idea why a quarter would be like that. I know now she hadn't been telling me the truth; she knew very well what it was but was trying to shield me from some anti-Catholicism.

Anyway, I hung onto it because it was so weird-looking.

Steppenwolf's new song "Born to Be Wild" was playing on my stereo one Saturday afternoon as I was fingering the coins in my bank.

That's when, stumbling upon this quarter, I cooked up my great idea.

Or I guess I should say my horrible idea.

Gazing at the red on that coin, I realized that if I got Markette expelled, I wouldn't have to deal with her anymore. Not with her looks, not with her brains, not with her better report cards, and especially not with her getting between me and my crush Tony, not that she'd reciprocated his interest.

The left corner of my mouth curled up in a crooked smile. After all, Tony couldn't be entranced by a girl who wasn't there.

That Monday I put the first phase of my evil scheme into action. I checked a few random books out of the school library and held onto them until a fine was due. I didn't bother to read them. That's not what they were for.

During the next week after they were overdue, I paid the fines for them one day at a time at the beginning of the lunch hour. I hoped to get an afternoon Sister Thomas forgot to show up for the second shift at the library. Each time I handed Sister Angela a regular quarter, but my plan was to sneak the red one into Markette's desk and claim I'd paid with that one.

The third time I returned a book, I got lucky. I paid a fine to Sister Angela at the beginning of lunch, which made her a witness to me handing her a quarter. Later on, Sister Thomas didn't show. I waited until Sister Angela left the circulation desk unattended to slip behind the counter and grab the money myself.

Well, you know what happened. Boy, did I pick the wrong day! You know of course that Markette was in the convent with Sister Thomas. It had not even occurred to me to check if Markette was in the library that day. I had just figured that, like always, she would have been. So, there was no way I could have known she wasn't there when I robbed the library fund.

Before the bell rang to end lunch, I snuck the money, along with the red quarter, into her desk.

Because of my insistence about the red quarter

and because hot embarrassment flooded my cheeks, I'm sure it was obvious to everyone, including Sister Angela, that I was the guilty party.

But wouldn't you know—of all people, the person I had framed came to my rescue by saying anybody could have planted the money.

I was relieved I wasn't going to be punished. Still, sitting at my desk, I clenched my jaw. My plan had backfired so badly that I had raised Markette's status in the eyes of the other students while at the same time diminishing my own.

26

I did want to get rid of Markette but not the way it happened.

Honestly, I didn't want her to die. I just wanted her out of my life as much as possible. I finally resolved myself to the fact that once we started ninth grade at our local junior high, we would not have the same classes all the time, and I could avoid her irritating presence for the most part.

You're probably wondering, then, why Verna, Damara, and I played keep-away with her report card. Well, I'll tell you.

Markette was standing at the corner of Main and Elm, waiting for the light to change. She happened to be gazing at her report card.

I had busted my butt earning straight A's that last term. Finally, my report card would not come up short in comparison. When I saw Markette checking hers, I grabbed it to take a look.

I was hoping she had at least one A-, or, even better, a B+.

That's when my eyes widened in astonishment at the A+.

Oh, no. I could hear Mom now: "Markette got an A+. Why didn't you get an A+?"

I had gotten a perfect report card, yet she had still managed to outshine me!

I can't begin to tell you how ticked I was. Acid boiled in my stomach. I remember clenching my jaw, hard, as I passed the card to Verna, who passed it to Damara. I didn't want Markette to have it, not a report card with a grade like that!

We were almost to the opposite corner when I held it high, just out of her reach. "You want it? Go get it!"

Honestly, I didn't stop to think what the consequences could be when I tossed it into the air. I didn't think about how dangerous it was to do that in the intersection of two busy main streets.

We three girls were laughing hysterically as we stepped onto the curb. A few of our steps later came a horrible screech of tires, a thud I can never put out of my mind, and a woman screaming.

We instantly turned around but stood frozen at the sight of a red sports car stopped a few feet beyond the crosswalk. Oh my God. Oh no.

No, no, no!

A woman yelled, "Somebody call an ambulance!"

I couldn't see Markette's body. The sports car was in the way. I'd already been sick to my stomach about her grades, but now a heavy queasiness surged through me. The three of us ran back, but at the corner a young brown-haired man stepped before us with outstretched arms.

"You don't want to see it," he said, shielding us.

Part of me wanted to look, make sure she was okay. At the same time, I didn't want to look because—

What if it was so bad that I really wouldn't want to see it? What if it was an image I didn't want to carry with me the rest of my life?

Damara's voice quivered. "Is she all right?"

"Just stay here," the man said, continuing to block our way.

We three held onto each other.

The woman who had been driving the sports car got out, had one glimpse of Markette, then dropped to her knees and started screaming over and over. Two men approached her from behind and, grasping her under her arms, led her away.

My heart pounded. I prayed *Dear God, let her be all right. Please, please, please! I'll do anything You want. I'll do anything You ask. Please let her be okay! Let her get up and walk over here. I'll never pick on her again, I promise!*

It seemed to take forever for the ambulance to arrive. At long last sirens wailed, but they were from two police cruisers that braked to a halt. A crowd began to gather. Occasionally a person would take a glimpse, wince, and look away. One of the police officers scooped a sheet out of his patrol car. I could see through the windows of the red car that he was laying it out.

Please let that be to keep her warm, I prayed. Please don't let it be—No! Don't let that happen!

My sleeve started feeling damp as the ambulance arrived. Damara, her face buried in my shoulder, was weeping.

After what seemed like forever, the rear of the ambulance was opened, and a gurney yanked out. Moments later, we saw what we were dreading: a body, completely covered, being lifted inside.

I forcefully broke away from Verna and

Damara, and ran. I ran toward home like a madman. I wanted to get away from it, like it had never happened.

I bolted the three blocks to my house and crashed into the kitchen.

Mom took one look at me and gasped, "What's wrong?"

How could I tell her? How could I tell my mother Markette was dead? How could I tell her I was responsible?

Leaning over, I retched on the kitchen floor.

Then I passed out.

* * *

Later I didn't recall the rest of that day except for a few flashes of memory. I think I was too numb. I remember Mom shaking me awake, concern in her eyes. Then the scene jumped to her on the phone commiserating with someone or the other, saying, "Oh my! Isn't it just awful?"

She must have gotten some information about the accident because at one point she hugged me and said, "Thank God you were out of the way before that car hit! I could have lost you too!"

I stiffened like a statue. I didn't want her to hug me.

I didn't deserve to be hugged.

The next morning when I woke up, for a second everything was all right. My bedroom looked the same: desk, window, Beatles poster.

Then I remembered.

The knowledge was a rock of darkness lodged in my heart.

Like a zombie I descended the stairs and found Mom in the kitchen. "Tell me it didn't happen. Tell me I dreamed it. Tell me it was a nightmare."

Mom gazed at me, pity in her eyes. "Oh, honey, I can't tell you that."

My butt painfully hit a kitchen chair as I sat down before I fell down.

All I could do was stare into space.

I could not undo the past.

That rock, I knew, was destined to be imbedded in my heart the rest of my life.

27

The funeral was the last place I wanted to be. Despite my protests, my abject begging, my parents told me I had to go. Mom even took me shopping and bought a black dress for me to wear to it, although I didn't bother checking in the store mirror to see how it looked.

Staring at myself in a mirror was one of the last things I wanted to do.

In the living room as she, Dad, and I were about to leave, I once again pleaded to be excused.

Dad said, "How will it look if you're not there at the funeral of a good, close friend?

My insides twisted at him calling Markette "a good, close friend." It was hardly how I had treated her.

"Why can't you just tell people I'm sick?"

I was sick. I was an emotional wreck. It'd been a little over a week, and I'd lost six pounds. I couldn't eat. I couldn't sleep.

And that rock embedded in my heart wouldn't go away.

Dad put on his glasses. "You are coming with us," he said firmly, clasping his hand on my shoulder and leading me to the car.

Wouldn't you know we had to drive through the intersection of Main and Elm to get to the church? I couldn't help staring at that spot near the curb, almost as if it were hypnotizing me. It was all cleaned up now, like nothing had happened.

I wished I could be all cleaned up like nothing had happened. I wished I could feel normal again.

Then it occurred to me that I hadn't felt normal since I'd punched Markette in the nose.

When we arrived at the church, I didn't want to see the casket, but it was impossible to miss. There, right in the space in front of the pews was the evidence of my guilt.

My knees collapsed. Mom and Dad had to pick me up.

After we were settled in our pew, I concentrated on cleaning my nails. I had to look at anything else and do anything else rather than what I was being forced to do.

Mom passed me a pamphlet with Markette's smiling face on it. Oh, this was the last thing I needed! Markette Maria Mason. January 22, 1954 – June 14, 1968. I immediately set it aside.

Verna and Damara scooted in behind me.

Damara whispered, "Scarlet? You okay?"

I shook my head a bit.

Mom shooed them back to their families.

During the rest of the funeral two scenes kept agonizingly replaying in my mind: *Why don't you do the world a favor? Why don't you just drop dead?* and *You want it? Go get it!*

I sat there, catatonic to everything around me, giving myself the cleanest nails in history.

If only my heart could have been that clean.

* * *

Guess where the reception after the funeral was held.

Right. You probably don't have to guess. We Hansens had the biggest house of all our friends, so Mom had volunteered our place for it.

I managed to beg off going to the burial by telling my folks it would be too much for me, which was the truth. Thank goodness they let me snag a ride with Verna's folks.

The moment I got home, I dashed upstairs to my room like the devil was chasing me. I did not want to be in the kitchen, where all the catered food—canapes and little triangular sandwiches—was laid out. Watching people eat would probably make me puke. I also didn't want to be in the living room where everybody would be talking about Markette, about how wonderful she was.

Yeah, how wonderful she *was*. Past tense.

I especially didn't want to see Mr. and Mrs. Mason when they eventually arrived from the burial. How could I look at them, see the grief on their faces? How could I even be in the same room with them? I had managed to completely avoid them at the funeral, but that would be impossible downstairs.

My bedroom was as far away as I could get.

A soft knock rapped on my door. I recognized Verna's voice. "Scarlet? You in there?"

I said nothing. My room was the same it had been before all this had happened: pink bedspread, reading lamp and princess phone on the desk. How I wished I could go back in time to the day I'd moved in here. As I sat on my bed, my nails got incredibly interesting again.

The door opened a slit. "Damara's here with me. Is it okay if we come in?"

"No," I said. "Yes. No. No. Yes."

They took that for permission and scooted onto the bed, one on either side at the foot.

"It's not your fault," Damara said. "That woman ran a red light. The police even arrested her for . . . what's it called?"

Verna said, "It's called involuntary vehicular manslaughter."

I winced. I knew they were trying to help, but this was something else to feel guilty about. If Markette had cleared the intersection, that lady would have only run a red light and maybe gotten a ticket instead of facing a possible prison term.

You want it? Go get it!

I sucked in a deep breath. "She dropped her report card, right? That's why she went after it."

I gazed up at them. Verna, concern in her eyes, swallowed hard.

Damara said, "I didn't see what happened with it. I was turned away."

"That's what happened," I said. "She dropped it."

Verna said, "Um . . . "

I gathered up all the strength I had in me and forced it into one sentence. "She dropped it!"

"Okay. If you say so," Verna said. "She dropped it."

I held up my right little finger. "Pinkie swear."

Damara didn't seem to have too much trouble wrapping her finger around mine. I guess in her mind, because she hadn't seen what I had done, it was easier for her. Verna hesitated a moment, then complied.

"If anybody asks, she dropped it," I said.

The rock in my heart tightened.

* * *

I spent most of that summer in my room. I didn't go into the pool once; it was too much of a reminder. Just about everything was a reminder. The place in the living room where I'd punched Markette in the nose. The kitchen table where we'd played Candy Land.

Most of all, the corner of Main and Elm.

I started having nightmares. I had a recurring dream in which Markette appeared to me, all grown up and cradling an armful of white lilies glowing with light.

"These are for you," she said. "One for each time you bullied me but I forgave you."

Oh, my goodness, there were so many! But I didn't want to be forgiven. I didn't deserve to be forgiven. I slapped the flowers out of her arms and screamed, "Leave me alone!"

I was relieved when school started. School and studying were a blessed distraction. And, thank God! although I did have to cross Elm to walk to the junior high, it was on our side of Main Street, so I crossed at a different intersection.

Another distraction was my parents' liquor cabinet.

Somehow Mom never noticed the vodka was slowly depleting and getting watered down. I also found out at school where I could get drugs, and a lot of my babysitting money—and sometimes even cash out of my parents' wallets—went to that.

I would do *anything* to relieve the cold darkness in my heart.

Including sex.

I wasn't quite sixteen when I lost my virginity in the backseat of a car. I barely knew the boy but didn't care. He said he loved me, and I was desperate to be loved. Maybe giving him what he wanted, I reasoned, would make him love me more, make me feel better about myself.

It didn't. It only made me feel worse, especially when he dumped me immediately afterward.

I was lucky I didn't get pregnant. Or an STD.

Then one afternoon in my room, I was listening to my stereo radio when a song by Paul Revere and the Raiders was broadcast. The lyrics of "Kicks" talked about how, even after trying one kind of kicks after another, you'd still be the same person with the same problem.

I'd heard the song before. It had been out a few years. But this time it was like a slap in the face, a wake-up call.

I managed to wean myself off the drugs and alcohol.

One gloomy overcast Sunday when we went to church, I got down on my knees and prayed *God, You can do anything. Please take away this rock in my heart. In return, I will do anything You ask. I'll even die, if that's what it takes.*

Silence.

Maybe God wasn't listening to me.
Maybe I didn't deserve to be listened to.
I certainly didn't deserve any special favors.

28

Most of my high school years were spent in a state of deep depression. Well, what did I have to look forward to but a lifetime of this heaviness inside? I even contemplated suicide, but that, I knew, would devastate my parents beyond belief. Creating more grief and sorrow over a death was not something I was willing to do.

One evening while I was studying, I heard Mom and Dad downstairs in the living room, bickering loudly enough that I could hear them.

"I'm telling you something is really bothering Scarlet!" Mom yelled.

Dad asked, "Like what?"

"I don't know. I can't get her to talk to me."

Well, duh. Like I was going to tell them what I'd done.

"I know she's been a bit down lately—" Dad began.

"A bit down? I think we're talking full-blown depression here. When is the last time you saw her smile? She spends all her free time in her room, won't call any of her friends, doesn't date, and barely eats even her favorite foods. Honestly, I think she may need professional help."

"Oh, you women are always exaggerating. It's probably just hormones."

"And you men are always blaming our moods on that, as if women can't be upset for any other reason!"

"Honey, I am telling you it's just teenage angst. Besides, how would it look if it got around that a respected doctor's daughter was seeing a psychiatrist?"

Yeah, that was the way Dad saw things. What other people would think was the ultimate in importance.

From there the argument heated into name-calling and slamming doors.

And I was no better off.

In fact, I was worse because now my guilt was affecting my parents too.

* * *

February 9th of my junior year, I got a rude awakening.

All of southern California got a rude awakening.

I'd once again been having that dream about Markette bringing me lilies when at about six in the morning a loud rumbling and the bed shaking thrust me out of sleep in an instant. As adrenaline spurt through my veins, I flung the bedcovers off and bolted for the doorway. We'd all been told the doorway was the safest place in an earthquake although now I understand that wouldn't have helped much, and I would have been better off diving under my desk.

I held onto the jamb for dear life as the whole house rattled. My desk lamp crashed to the floor, and the shoe rack in my closet tilted over. Through my bedroom window I glimpsed a power line pole violently rocking back and forth, sparks shooting from its transformer.

This is it! I thought, the floor rippling under my bare feet. *We're all going to die!*

By the time the tremors subsided, I was so scared my vision momentarily faded into blindness. My sight, fortunately, returned by the time my parents dashed down the upstairs hall toward me.

"Are you all right?" Mom asked.

"Yeah." Well, as all right as I usually was, considering.

Mom, Dad, and I flew down the stairs and turned on the television. News coverage began detailing the damage. Some bridges were down. Part of a hospital had collapsed. We soon learned that the magnitude was 6.6 on the Richter scale.

My arms hugged my waist. I could have died. I could have died right then and there.

Died with that heaviness still in my heart.

It should have been another wake-up call for me, but I got distracted by an announcement that all schools were closed for the day until any damage could be assessed.

All right! A day off from school. I would definitely take that.

The next few hours were spent glued to the TV and answering the phone from friends and relatives who were calling to be sure we were okay.

After she hung up from one such call, Mom said, "That was Verna's mother. Most of the books at the public library were knocked off the shelves. Verna is going over there to help. Don't you think you should go with her and help too?"

Actually, I had been thinking about going

upstairs and listening to my new Partridge Family album. I'd thrown over Paul McCartney in favor of a crush on David Cassidy. Distractions from my conscience were what I was currently living for.

"But—" I began. It was as far as I got.

"You," Mom said, "are old enough to start helping your community in at least some small way when a disaster strikes."

From the sternness in Mom's eyes and the tightness of her lips, I knew there would be no getting out of this.

So Verna and I walked over to the library to volunteer. Fortunately, this did not entail crossing either Main or Elm.

Oh, my goodness! I thought as we stepped inside the building. Was there a volume remaining on a shelf? We would practically have to wade through mounds of books to even begin. And, not only would they have to go onto the shelves, they had to go in the right Dewey Decimal order.

Even with the librarians and other volunteers helping, this was going to take all day. Someone brought in a transistor radio, and we listened to the constant newscasts as we set about putting the library back in order.

Verna and I started in the biography section. I sat on the floor and handed her one book after another. We'd only gotten about ten books in when Verna stopped, frozen, with a book in her hand.

"What's wrong?" I asked.

She glanced at me. "What does this remind you of?"

I shrugged. "Nothing in particular. Why? Does it remind you of something?"

"You don't remember? In the school library. How we knocked the books off the shelves and blamed it on Markette. And how she stayed after school to clean it up."

"Oh." I frowned. I had forgotten about that.

I had been very happy to forget about that.

For a moment Verna and I stared at each other. "Well," she said, "maybe this can be our way of kind of making up for it."

I hadn't thought about that before, about making up for what I'd done. Yeah, maybe this, in God's eyes, would help make amends for that one incident.

But how on earth could I make up for Markette's death?

29

Of course I couldn't make atonement for Markette's death, no matter what I did and no matter how hard I tried. Only Christ's death could suffice for that.

That night in bed I thought about it while I once again stared at the dark ceiling of my room. Wouldn't some sort of penance show God how badly I wanted to change? Since Christ atoned for our sins, shouldn't I also make some sort of reparation in order to be Christ-like?

Wouldn't that count for something? I wondered.

Even if it did, what would be enough for something so awful as putting Markette in mortal danger by flinging her report card into the air in a busy intersection?

I sighed, rolling onto my left side. I had no idea what I could do.

By the time I was a high school senior I had learned to accept that the dark heavy guilt eating away at me was the way things were, the way they were always going to be.

Amazingly, I was able to keep my grades up. One thing the competition with Markette had taught me was how to study. Besides, I would have really heard about it from Mom and Dad if I didn't. I was expected, after all, to be the first female doctor in my family. I was disappointed enough in myself. I didn't need them disappointed in me too.

June 14, 1972, the last day of high school,

Verna, Damara, and I walked home. It was a typical sunny California afternoon, the sky a bright blue. I said goodbye to them at their homes down the street, then continued toward mine.

A glance at my report card provoked a smile, although I didn't smile often. I'd managed straight A's again, although I wasn't the school valedictorian. Nope, a B+ in English junior year was making me salutatorian, which even Dad had accepted, although reluctantly. Personally, I blamed Shakespeare and *Macbeth* for keeping me out of the top spot.

This afternoon all I had to do was cross the suburban avenue in front of our house and go inside in order to get a whole lot of praise from my mom.

That's when I saw her, a little brown-haired girl, no more than three-years-old, walking all by herself right in the middle of the intersection. The speed limit was 25, but a car was racing toward her.

Everything in me screamed "Go!"

I automatically dropped what was in my hands and raced into the street, scooping up the child as I dashed toward the opposite curb. The car zoomed by so closely the wind from its passing blew my clothes. Whoever was driving obviously wasn't paying enough attention to even slow down or touch the brakes.

I carried the little girl to the sidewalk and set her down. I sank to my knees so I would be closer to eye-level with her. "Where is your mother?"

She stared at me blankly.

She did look like she might be Hispanic, so I

summoned up what little I remembered of my two years of Spanish.

"*¿Dónde está tu madre?*" Where is your mother?

"*No sé.*" I don't know.

Sighing, I rose, picked her up, and brought her into the house. Well, I could hardly leave her on the street, could I? She might walk right back into the intersection.

"Mom!" I called, setting the child down in the kitchen.

The house was quiet, deathly quiet. Oh, that's right. She'd told me she was going to be out shopping this afternoon.

I picked up the phone and called the new 911 emergency line.

"I was walking home from school, and I found this little girl wandering the street," I explained. "She almost got hit by a car."

"Where is she now?" the female operator asked.

"I brought her inside my house so she'll be safe."

"Can you describe her?"

"Um, sure. She's about three, and she's wearing jeans and a red shirt with Scooby-Doo on it. She doesn't seem to speak any English, but I did talk to her a bit in Spanish."

"Can you ask her what her name is?"

"Um, sure. Hold on a minute. *¿Cómo te llamas?*"

"Maria."

"She says her name is Maria."

"We've been looking for that little girl for some time," the operator said. "And what is your name?"

"Scarlet Hansen."

"Scarlet, would you please take care of her until we can send someone out?"

"Sure, no problem. I babysit all the time." I supplied my address to the operator and hung up.

I brought Maria out to the front porch and sat down with her. She gave me a smile and a hug.

Five minutes later a police cruiser pulled up, and both the officer and a woman who looked like a grown-up Maria stepped out.

"Mama!" the girl squealed.

The woman opened her arms wide. "Maria!" she cried, scooping her up and kissing her all over.

I grinned as the woman kept telling me "Gracias, gracias," plus a flurry of words in Spanish spoken way too fast for me to translate.

The police officer took my statement.

As they pulled away, I suddenly remembered. My report card! I had dropped it in order to have my hands free when I had rushed into the street.

There it was, caught in a bush across the street and flapping a bit in the mild breeze.

As I brought it inside, I thought this afternoon's events had certainly been the most amazing thing that had happened to me.

Well, at least the most amazing thing that day.

I was wrong.

I was more wrong than I could possibly have imagined.

* * *

Cookies and milk were always my best choice for an after-school snack. We had chocolate chip, my favorite, so I set a couple of them on a bread plate and poured myself a cold glass of milk.

It was while I was standing with my back leaning against the kitchen sink and raising my glass to take a gulp that it hit me.

A report card in the street.

A car rushing toward a girl in an intersection.

The girl's name was Maria, and Markette's middle name was Maria.

Today was June 14, the anniversary of Markette's death.

The glass slipped from my hand and crashed to the floor, milk and shards of glass spreading over the linoleum. My knees buckled, and I soon joined the mess on the floor, screaming.

Tears blinded me. Somewhere in the back of my mind, I realized this was the first time I'd cried about Markette's death.

One wave of anguish rolled out of me after another, to be replaced by yet another, and another, like surf crashing on a shore.

"I'm sorry!" I cried. "Dear God, I'm so sorry! I'm sorry for all of it!"

What happened next is hard to explain, but I'll try.

Brilliant light flooded from a corner of the kitchen. Blinding as it normally would be, it didn't hurt my eyes.

There, standing in the middle of the light, was Markette.

She was all grown-up, light blazing from her form. I had never seen anyone so beautiful, and her arms were full of lilies shining with an unearthly light.

Just like in the dream I kept having.

I blinked. Was I hallucinating? Was I so emotionally distraught that I was seeing things?

"Markette?" I managed to get out of my mouth.

Her smile was amazingly lovely. "You can see me?"

I nodded.

"I've tried appearing to you before."

"You have?"

"You kept blocking me. I was trying to bring you some lilies. One for each time you bullied me, to show you I've forgiven you."

My mouth dropped open. "That was really you? In those dreams?"

"Yes. So now you've finally opened up enough that God is permitting you to see and hear me."

"It was all the coincidences," I said, "The little girl, the report card . . . "

"There are no coincidences with God."

"It was all planned?"

She laughed, and her laughter was like music. "Not planned. *Foreseen.* God knew exactly what was going to happen, so He prompted me to step inside you and shout 'Go!' when you saw the little girl in danger."

"That was you? I thought it was my own idea."

"It was both of ours. And now I've come to tell you God has a plan for you. You've prayed that you can show Him how sorry you are? You've asked Him what you can do to make up for everything? He's answering your prayer by calling you on a special mission."

This next part is also difficult to articulate, but in an instant I understood what I was meant to do.

"You have a lot to go through to prepare for that," Markette said. "But I'll be there, at your side, even if you can't see or hear me."

She and the light started to fade.

"Wait!" I cried. "Don't go!"

"This isn't goodbye. This is 'I'll see you later.' I promise to be there, waiting for you, when you arrive on the other side."

With that, she was gone. Or, at least, I couldn't see or hear her anymore.

I sat there like an idiot.

I put my hand over my chest.

The lump was still there, but it wasn't anywhere near as hard as before.

30

I knew the first thing I had to do was going to be the hardest.

I had to own up to what I had done.

After I cleaned up the glass and milk on the kitchen floor, I headed upstairs to my bedroom. Sitting on my bed, a pillow clutched over my stomach, I called Verna and Damara from my princess phone and told them the pinkie swear we'd made after Markette died was no longer in effect. I was going to come clean about the bullying.

"Um, okay," Verna told me over the wire. "But does this mean you're going to mention my involvement?"

"No," I said. "That's your own story to tell. But I do want to apologize for dragging you down into it."

"Yeah, we could have been a little nicer."

Well, that was one rather insufficient way of putting it.

"*Should* have been nicer," I told her. "A whole lot nicer."

Damara was much more open to my phone call. Maybe this whole thing was easier for her because she hadn't actually seen me toss Markette's report card into the air. I admit I kind of envied her having her conscience more clear than mine.

"I'm so glad you're doing this," she said. "I think it's a wonderful idea. You're going to feel so much better afterward."

"Maybe so, but I won't feel so great *doing* it," I said.

* * *

Talking to my parents would be tougher. I was, I knew, going to completely shatter their image of me as their wonderful daughter.

I decided to wait until after dinner, which was probably a mistake. How could I eat anything when I knew what was coming? The mashed potato dam holding back my gravy was not only broken by my fork but smeared all over my plate. I don't think any of it made it into my mouth.

When the dishwasher was finally humming, I called both of them into the living room. Staring at me expectantly, they took the sofa while I sat facing them on the loveseat.

Staring back, I gulped, hard. My insides were liquifying into jelly. Mom, with her red frizzy hair just like mine, Dad with strands of gray at his temples. I opened my mouth, but nothing would come out.

Dad removed his glasses and frowned. "So what's this all about? You look so serious. UCLA hasn't rescinded your acceptance, has it?"

"No. Nothing like that," I said. It occurred to me that I could soften the blow by first telling them about the little girl Maria and how I had saved her life, so I started with that.

"Oh, my goodness!" Mom cried when I was finished. Both of her hands covered her mouth. "What were you thinking, running into the street in front of a speeding car? You could have been killed!"

Dad, however, was all smiles. "Evelyn! Do you realize what this means? Our daughter's a hero! Wait'll everybody hears about this!"

Well, that was typical. Mom concerned for my safety, Dad concerned what people would think.

I hung my head. "I'd prefer it if you didn't say anything about it."

Dad was already on his feet. "Well, why not? They should probably give you a medal at City Hall or something!"

For a moment I gritted my teeth and clasped my sweaty palms. Then I said, "You don't understand. I wouldn't deserve it."

"Why not?" Dad cried.

"Because . . . because of Markette." There. I had at least gotten her name out.

This produced some frowning on their part. Mom asked, "What does Markette have to do with any of this?"

My hands were so tightly clasped my nails were digging into my flesh. "I guess I should start by telling you . . . I lied."

"About?" Dad prompted.

"About saying I didn't break her nose. I'm the one who broke it. I punched her in the face."

Mom jumped to her feet too. "Wha . . . wha . . . why would you do such a thing?"

I clamped my mouth shut. I want you to know how tempted I was, so sorely tempted to point at her and say something like *It's* your *fault! You said her nose was pretty and mine was ugly! You're the one who started all this!*

But I had made my own choices. True, I hadn't fully understood what I'd been doing when I was a little five-year-old child. I had certainly understood later, though. And I had chosen the wrong path over and over again.

What I said was, "I was jealous. Her nose was prettier than mine."

For a second Mom's jaw dropped. Then she said, "Why on earth would you think a silly thing like that?"

I sighed. Obviously, she didn't remember what she'd said that fateful day almost thirteen years ago. I was glad I had kept my mouth shut. Pointing it out would only serve to make her feel horrible, and she was already going to feel completely devastated by the time I was finished.

Dad changed the subject. "We," he said, "are incredibly lucky the Masons didn't know this. They could have sued us. They sued the butt off that woman who hit Markette with her car."

I sucked in a painful breath. "About that . . ." I began.

I'll spare you the sordid details. By the end of it, I was crying hysterically. Mom, bless her, threw her arms around me in a hug, saying she still loved me and would always love me, no matter what.

Dad, however, was back on the sofa, fuming.

By the time Mom let go, I was crying so hard I started hiccupping. "I have to tell the Masons," I said. "I have to apologize to them."

"Now that," Dad snarled, pointing his finger at

me, "you are not going to do. Do you have any idea what kind of financial ramification that could have? They won't hesitate to sue us! Even if we won, we'd still have all the lawyer fees, not to mention the damage to my reputation!"

"But I have to! Don't you understand, Daddy? I have to come clean!"

"I understand why you want to, but I'm afraid you can't," Mom said. "They moved. Mr. Mason inherited a fortune, and they both left. The last I heard they were touring Europe, but I have no idea where. Mrs. Mason and I, well, we sort of drifted apart . . . "

"Because you still have your daughter and they don't," I finished for her. "And being around you, and especially around me, would be too painful."

Mom was silent, but I knew I had hit the nail on the head. Great, just great. Tears streaking my cheeks, I realized I had destroyed years of friendship between two former high school girls. Was there no end to the dark ripples my actions had caused?

Grabbing several tissues, I wiped the tears away. I allowed them several minutes to calm down before I continued. "There's more."

"Oh, now what?" Dad cried.

I crossed to the sofa, sat next to my father, and laid my hand on his. "Daddy, I know your work is very important. You fight disease. You fix what's wrong inside people's bodies, and that's wonderful. But I want to do something even better."

Dad slipped his glasses back on. "And what

would that be?" he asked, frowning as if he couldn't imagine anything more dignified than being a medical doctor.

"I want to fight evil. Specifically, evil against children."

His jaw clenched. "My daughter," he said, "is going to be a surgeon. I decided that the day you were born. I have been raising you for that ever since."

"Daddy, this is something I have to do, something I think God wants me to do. I have to make up for all the things I've done, all the times I bullied Markette."

I guess he saw the determination in my eyes, because he let out a huge sigh. "If you really want to work with children, I guess you could be a pediatric surgeon."

"Daddy, that's not what I have in mind. I'm going to spend my life helping abused children."

"No. What will people think if you end up as nothing more than a social worker?"

As if being a social worker was beneath me. As if what other people thought was more important than helping a little kid in distress. In my mind I envisioned those children, hundreds of them battered and bruised, reaching out their arms to me, begging for help.

What was I supposed to say to them? Something like "Sorry, but disappointing my father is more important than helping you"?

I was about to object to Dad's comments when Mom jumped in. "Wait! I have an idea. What if

Scarlet becomes a lawyer? What if she becomes a prosecutor? What if she prosecutes child abuse cases?"

I stared into Dad's blue eyes. Would that be prestigious enough to satisfy him?

He let out his breath. "I suppose if you have to."

31

That Saturday afternoon I walked to the church, rain splattering the sidewalks. It was unusual weather for that time of year in southern California, but I didn't bother with an umbrella. Maybe I saw getting soaked as a penance of sorts. Drops showering upon me made it seem like the whole sky was weeping, especially when I arrived at the intersection of Main and Elm. It was the only way I could safely walk to the church. I admit I crossed Elm first, then Main, even though it meant sloshing through a puddle, cold rain soaking the socks inside my shoes. I wanted to avoid the spot where Markette had died. I couldn't quite bring myself to step there.

Coming clean with my parents was one thing. I had to come clean with God.

As I walked along, rain drenching my clothes and clinging them to my skin, I knew God was already fully aware of everything I'd done. He already knew I was sorry, wanted to be forgiven, and of course He was ready to forgive me.

Whatever you think about sacramental Confession, let me tell you: you really own up to what you've done when you say it out loud. Maybe that's why James 5:16 commands that we not only pray for one another but that we should also confess our sins to one another.

I wrung out my long red hair as best as I could before entering through the church's heavy back door. I slid into line in a pew where three other penitents were already waiting to confess. Sitting there, I was a bit of a nervous wreck in the dark church, heavy rain pattering on the roof. But, staring at the front of the nave, I remembered the day I'd walked in and seen Markette's casket.

You can do this, I told myself, gathering my courage from deep down inside.

When the light over the confessional changed from red to green, finally indicating it was my turn, I forced one foot in front of the other until I made it into the booth, closed the door, and knelt. The moment the screen between the priest and me opened, I began, "Bless me, Father, for I have sinned. It's been . . . I don't remember how long it's been since my last confession."

"Years?" he prompted through the screen.

"Lot of years," I admitted. "I want to confess, but I'm not sure I remember how."

Father, bless him, said, "In that case, let me help you with this." And he proceeded to take me one at a time through the Ten Commandments, asking questions along the way.

Oh! There was so much to get off my chest! It wasn't only what I'd done to Markette, but all the lying, the cheating, the alcohol, the drugs, and, yes, that incident in the backseat of a car when I'd gone way too far with that boy. I don't know what the people behind me in line were thinking about me taking so long, but then I realized it didn't matter.

Father had to talk me through the prayer The Act of Contrition because I didn't remember it either. But when he pronounced absolution, oh! I actually felt, physically, an incredible weight lift off me.

You may think that was psychosomatic. Well, maybe, but it took me so by surprise that I think there was more to it.

The penance Father gave me was to go out and do a good deed for someone. That was one penance I was sure I'd be glad to do!

Afterward, I knelt in the church, gazing up at the crucifix over the altar. "Thank you," I whispered, staring at the image of Christ in death. "Thank you so much for going through so much to forgive me so much."

It wasn't until I rose from my knees to leave that I noticed the heaviness in my heart was gone.

As I placed my hand over my chest, I couldn't help recalling words from the thirty-sixth chapter of Ezekiel: *And I will give you a new heart, and put a new spirit within you: and I will take away the stony heart out of your flesh, and will give you a heart of flesh. And I will put my spirit in the midst of you: and I will cause you to walk in my commandments, and to keep my judgments, and do them.*

* * *

Every night, for four years of college and three years of law school, I stared in the dark at my bedroom ceiling and recalled the vision I'd had of Markette. I didn't tell anyone about it, of course. I didn't want people to think I was crazy, but I'm okay telling you it happened because now that I'm dead, it doesn't matter what people think.

What people did think at the time was that I was brilliant. I threw myself into my studies, pretty much forgoing any kind of social life, including dating. Whereas before I'd had crushes on boys, now my sole focus was on becoming the best attorney I could be.

All the studying paid off. I graduated from UCLA *magna cum laude*, then third in my class at USC law school. Even Dad, who hadn't been too happy about my career choice, was proud, even proud enough to brag to his friends.

A lot of people were surprised when I applied to the District Attorney's Office in the county of Los Angeles. After all, with college credentials like mine, I could have made thousands of dollars more working in the private sector for a law firm. Anyway, I became Scarlet Ann Hansen, Assistant District Attorney for the county of Los Angeles.

I volunteered to prosecute child abuse cases, even though these are often the most difficult and heart-wrenching. Police and other prosecutors often have nightmares about the ugliness they see in our world, and I was having to deal with it on a daily basis when the victims were the most innocent of all.

Not only that, but I had to put children on the witness stand and have them relive the abuse by testifying about it. Oh, and I'd also have to watch the defense attorney try to tear some poor child's testimony apart.

And I knew I'd have only one chance to get a guilty verdict. If a defendant was found not guilty, double jeopardy forbid another prosecution. If I lost a case, unless some new, different charges were filed, that was it. Period.

Many evenings I drove home to my little one-bedroom apartment, threw myself on my bed, and cried my heart out. I knew I was supposed to be detached, to emotionally distance myself. But some children were so damaged either emotionally or physically—and often both—that I couldn't help myself.

So many times I wanted to quit. I got a case in which some parents had deliberately stirred rat poison into their son's baby food. Their plan was to claim the manufacturer had been negligent so they could sue for millions of dollars. I won easily because one thing those parents didn't know is that manufacturers as a matter of course keep samples of all batches. It was easy to test the baby food sample and prove it had been fine when the lids had been sealed on all the jars. But I was so devastated by a mother and father making their own baby so ill he almost died, I decided it would be my last prosecution.

That night I dreamed about Markette. There she was, blazing with light, her long brown hair blowing in a gentle breeze, her arms laden with pure white lilies.

"I am right here with you through all of it," she told me. "Don't give up. So many more children are awaiting your help."

By the morning, rather than being determined to quit, I was determined to continue.

So, continue I did. Often when I was stuck with a case, Markette would appear in my dreams to help. She'd do something like give me a question to ask a witness on the stand. The first time she did that, the question sounded so out of left field, I was more than a little hesitant, especially since it meant recalling a particular witness to the stand just to ask that one question. In court attorneys don't ask questions they don't already know the answers to. Trust me, one thing you don't want in court is a big surprise! In this particular case, a wrong answer would have made me look more than foolish in front of the judge and especially in front of the jury. In fact, it would have bolstered the defense's case. But I went ahead with it anyway, got the response I was hoping for, and it changed the entire outcome of the trial. Another time Markette told me about a witness, a family member we'd been unaware of because she had moved, and that person's testimony also produced a guilty verdict.

Because of the supernatural help, I started getting a reputation as one sharp prosecutor with a lot of convictions under my belt. But I was careful to give God the credit, although I don't think anybody believed me. Some of the other attorneys called it women's intuition; some called it lucky hunches.

I knew better.

One night Markette held out a single white lily to me and said, "Wait till you see the treasure you are storing up in heaven."

Dreams like that always bolstered me with the

strength to go on.

32

I was fifty-one years old and a seasoned prosecutor when my gray-haired boss, Brad Early, stopped by my desk. Amid all the clatter of the prosecutors' office, I glanced up at him, once again unable to help thinking how much he looked like the actor Ted Danson.

Brad closed the door to my office and handed me a file. "Take a look and tell me what you think."

My first thought when I saw the name George Thomas Davin on the tab was *Oh, no.*

Davin was a famous actor accused of abusing his thirteen-year-old daughter, often beating and starving her, locking her in closets, zip-tying her to her bed. Her mother, unfortunately, had died in childbirth, so the father was in charge of the girl by himself.

"Are you kidding me?" I asked Brad. "George Thomas Davin? Star of the wildly popular sit-com *World's Greatest Father* television show? No jury is going to believe the guy who plays the most beloved widowed dad on TV is an abuser. Everybody watches that show. I watch it myself."

"Check out the evidence," Brad said.

I flipped open the file. One glimpse of a photo of the girl in question, Margie Davin, was enough to squeeze my heart. Oh my goodness, if Markette had had a twin, this girl would be it. Brown bangs and a long braid. Big brown eyes with long lashes.

Yes, and a cute little button nose.

That's . . . quite a coincidence, I thought.

Then I remembered what Markette had told me: *There are no coincidences with God.*

I frowned. Was God trying to tell me something here? I hadn't had a dream about Markette for a while. Still, could it be that this case was especially important? All the victims were important to me, but could there be something distinctive about this one?

I shook my head, banishing the thought. I would give this case the same amount of attention I would any other, that is, all the attention I could muster.

Browsing through the file, I figured that one of Margie's teachers must have noticed some bruising because, as was required, her school had made a report to Child Protective Services, which had then begun an investigation. Reading further, I discovered there had probably been many witnesses to any abuse, but they had been illegal aliens of Davin's Bel Air household staff and were therefore reluctant to speak to anyone in authority.

Still, the media got wind of the fact that illegals were working for Davin, and that did make the national news. Since hiring illegals was not the best publicity for a well-known actor, Davin of course claimed he had been shocked—utterly *shocked* I tell you—to discover they were illegals. And so he had paid for them to return to Mexico, with nice fat additional bonuses to help them out once they arrived there.

My. How generous of him.

I commented, "Looks like he was bribing potential witnesses."

"Agreed," Brad said. "But impossible to prove."

Continuing in the file, I saw that one maid had bravely gone to the Mexican police, who in turn had contacted the LAPD. A couple of other servants had followed suit. I smiled. Davin had unwittingly given them no more reason to fear deportation and therefore not go to the authorities. That had certainly backfired on him.

It gave me a total of three willing to testify.

That raised my eyebrows. Three was a good number. I couldn't help thinking *Just like with Markette. The word of three against one. I like those odds.*

But there was a problem. "You realize," I told Brad, "all the witnesses, except for the child herself, are people who broke the law by entering the country illegally. The defense will use that little fact to taint their credibility. And that isn't even taking into account any bias a juror might already have toward illegal aliens. Or Hispanics, especially Hispanics testifying against a white man. A very prominent white man." I leaned back in my chair and shook my head a bit. "I don't know. This is hardly a slam-dunk."

"The LAPD," Brad said, sliding a VHS tape onto my desk, "has some lovely footage of Davin losing his temper when they interviewed him."

"Enough to look violent?"

"View it and decide for yourself. Do we have enough to move forward? Or should we drop the charges?"

A lot of cases are decided at this stage of the proceedings. If there's not enough evidence, there's no sense in spending the taxpayers' money on a trial that most likely will not result in a guilty verdict. Not only that, but a verdict of innocence would mean the perpetrator could not be tried for the same crime again, even if more evidence surfaced later. Sometimes waiting for more such evidence and a stronger case was the best option before proceeding to trial.

Which, unfortunately, meant the abuse might continue.

"I trust your judgment," Brad said.

"I assume Child Protective Services has removed the girl from the family home."

"Oh, yes."

I already knew from the television news that Davin was out on bail and claiming his innocence to any reporter who would listen.

"Let me know if you think you can win it," Brad said before heading out the door.

I sighed, popped the videotape into my office's player and turned on my TV.

33

After a moment of static and wavy distortion, the image on my office television settled into a picture of an LAPD interrogation room. The angle was from a camera mounted in a corner of the room, near the ceiling. It showed three persons sitting in three folding chairs, two of them LAPD detectives, and one of them George Thomas Davin.

I recognized Davin immediately by his brown crew-cut and the goofy smile on his face, the one he often mugged for the TV cameras. Because the camera showed the male detectives from behind, I couldn't see them as well. The image, as usual, was focused on the person being interviewed.

First Davin was read his rights. I recognized the voice of the detective reading them, Sergeant Rodriguez. Davin declined his right to have a lawyer present, claiming, "You guys are way off track" and "I have nothing to hide."

I smiled. This was a man who thought he was smarter than cops who had years of experience, as if he could, during his first time being interviewed, fool police officers who were well trained to detect lies. He was, apparently, relying on his TV persona to get him out of this. Big mistake.

"Guys," he said, spreading his arms wide, "this is all a misunderstanding. My daughter was upset about being grounded, so she made up these wild accusations."

That was the typical claim and blame strategy

that I recognized all too well from using it myself so many times. Claim innocence. Blame the victim.

"So," Rodriguez said, holding up a folder, "you didn't do any of this? Beat her? Zip-tie her to her bed?"

"Absolutely not!" Davin said.

Okay. Why was it whenever the police asked suspects if the charges were true, the reply was always "*Absolutely* not!" as if adding the adverb made it more true somehow.

It was exactly what I had told Sister Angela when she'd asked me if I'd thrown away Markette's lunch. One good thing about my experience at acting innocent when I was guilty was that I was able to recognize it when I saw it.

My eyes widened at a sudden realization. The fact that I, as a child, had been on the wrong side, ethically speaking, was turning out to be extremely beneficial in my work as a prosecutor. Yeah, that's how long it took me to comprehend that. Snorting, I admonished myself for being so slow on the uptake.

I couldn't help wondering if my bullying, or rather, my *repenting* of the bullying, was the reason why God had chosen me, of all people, for this kind of work. I had to admit I had been more than somewhat experienced at being nefarious, but it was the moment I had finally repented that Markette had appeared to me, telling me this would be my mission, my life's work.

Could be. It did make sense. The old saying was "It takes a thief to catch a thief." Did it, in a way, take a bully to catch a bully?

But, speaking of my life's work, I realized I needed to get back to it. I rewound the video to the place where Davin had declared his innocence, then continued the footage.

"How do you explain all the bruises?" Rodriguez asked.

Davin snorted and spread his arms wide. "She fell down the stairs."

"Did you take her to see a doctor?"

"She said she was fine."

That raised my eyebrows. His daughter had supposedly tumbled down some stairs, was injured enough to have bruises, and he was dismissing her injuries as inconsequential? Not even having her checked for a possible concussion?

I paused the interview and flipped through the file for the doctor's report made after CPS removed the child. Wow. Massive bruising, some of it weeks old. Inconsistent with one fall down some stairs.

The defense will try to argue those other bruises away, I mused, *probably by calling in some well-paid "expert witnesses."*

But maybe this actor wouldn't do so well when he didn't already have a script to follow . . . if I could get him on the witness stand. He didn't have to testify. The Fifth Amendment which protected Davin against double jeopardy also protected him against self-incrimination.

Staring at him paused on my TV screen, that smile plastered on his face, I figured he would probably insist on testifying, despite any advice from what were bound to be some very expensive, very experienced lawyers. This was the kind of man who would most likely try to charm the jury with the character he portrayed on TV.

He was an actor, after all. He knew how to play a part. Judging by the Emmy he had won last year, he was very good at it.

I hit Play and followed the interview for over two hours. I grew more and more confident that Davin would demand his right to testify. The man had an ego bigger than the galaxy. Everybody, he claimed, including the police, were out to get him. Everybody, he claimed, was lying.

Except him, of course.

Gradually he was losing his cool. Then the police asked Davin if there had been any sexual abuse. That, apparently, needled him so much that, his face bloated with anger, he snatched up his chair and slammed it across the room. I couldn't believe the words coming out of his mouth, ones definitely not fit for prime-time television.

Oh, that was just lovely.

But, I realized, *the defense will try to argue his belligerence away by saying he was exhausted and who wouldn't react that way after being questioned as a possible suspect of such a heinous crime?*

My eyes narrowed. *On the other hand, if I can provoke him enough that his temper explodes on the witness stand in front of the jury . . .*

Over the years I had gotten pretty darn good at doing just that sort of thing, even when I knew full well that the defense's lawyers had probably warned a witness that I would likely try to provoke him into losing his cool.

Still, I spent two days weighing the evidence and agonizing about whether or not to proceed with the case.

You know what decided me? Prayer.

"Markette," I breathed, "the Bible tells us that the prayer of the righteous availeth much. I know that you, now in heaven, must be righteous. Please ask God to help me with this one. Please ask Him to find a way to prove beyond a reasonable doubt—no, beyond *any* doubt—that this man is guilty. Please find a way I can save this poor child. Please, please, please somehow make this one a slam-dunk."

* * *

Pre-trial media coverage, as expected, was intense.

One evening I was watching the news in my apartment while devouring my Chinese take-out. I used a fork for that. Do you use chopsticks? I didn't know anybody who did except on television shows.

"My client is innocent," Stern Blakerly, Davin's famous and incredibly expensive attorney said on the courthouse steps as he clamped his hand on Davin's shoulder. The lawyer, with his perfectly cut brown hair and dark designer suit, looked like he had just stepped out of a men's fashion magazine. "We look forward to proving his innocence in court."

I couldn't help snorting, even with a mouthful of orange chicken. Ever notice how defense lawyers are always looking forward to proving their clients' innocence in court?

"This," he continued, "is nothing more than a witch hunt propagated by an overly ambitious prosecutor with political ambitions."

I gagged, nearly choking. *Hmmmm*, I mused. *I wonder what political ambitions I have. Strange. I wasn't aware of any.*

Grinning, I imagined myself phoning Blakerly and asking him exactly what my political ambitions were, since I'd really like to know. Of course I wouldn't do that, but it was fun to imagine him sputtering on the other end of the line.

The fact that there were no such ambitions made no difference. Once the idea was out there, what the man had said could not be unsaid. And the claim was going to be made, over and over again, on subsequent broadcasts that repeated the footage, including the national news.

I shook my head. It was a little too uncomfortably close to what I had done to Markette that day on the playground when I'd told her Linda had moved. I'd deliberately let her—and all the other girls—think the worst about her, even though I'd known it wasn't true.

Of course the public was only hearing one side. But I knew better than to go on camera where my words would be twisted, if not by the media, then by the defense.

Blakerly's slander had its effect. Almost instantly I was being crucified on social media. How dare I spread such vicious lies about the World's Greatest Father! How dare I try to send him to prison just to benefit myself and my supposed political career! The fact that my flaming red hair made me stand out also made me a well-known target. A few people managed to get my phone number, and I started getting death threats on my voice mail—which I, unfortunately, had to listen to so I could keep them as evidence, just in case.

I descended the stairs in front of my apartment one sunny morning to discover my little blue car vandalized: windows smashed, the enamel keyed, and a not very nice word that began with a B spray-painted on the side.

Brad arranged for the police to drive by my place a few times at night. Like that would help much.

One afternoon in the D.A.'s office he and I were discussing the case. The 5 o'clock national news started playing on a television in the background, and it got our attention when we heard Davin's name in the top story.

And there, in glorious color, was footage from the police interview, the part when Davin furiously hurled the chair across the room. As for what he said when the chair landed, well, almost all of that was bleeped . . . and bleeped and bleeped and bleeped.

"Oh, no!" I cried. "What idiot leaked that?"

Of course, the defense already knew about the interview. All evidence had to be handed over to Davin's lawyers. But there went my surprise—and evoking the emotional reaction it would cause the jurors—at showing this in court and unmasking the World's Greatest Father.

"Well," Brad said, "if nothing else, it should turn the tide in your favor."

Jurors, we knew, were supposed to be impartial, at least in theory. In practice, it was impossible. And now the national evening news had tainted a jury pool the size of the entire United States population.

A week later, due to the scandal, *World's Greatest Father* was canceled by its network.

That story made the national news too.

34

I got up the first morning of voir dire, the process of interviewing prospective jurors, and ate my usual breakfast of cereal and milk. Then I dressed in a white blouse and black skirt with a matching jacket before driving to the courthouse.

I parked my loaner car in my usual assigned space in the courthouse basement, but while crossing to the elevator, I heard a male voice call, "Miss Hansen!"

I turned around.

There was George Thomas Davin. Somehow he had managed to bypass security.

And he had a gun.

A gun pointed right at me.

My vision zoomed in on the end of the barrel.

"It's all your fault!" he screamed, his face bloated with the same red rage I'd seen on the videotape. The hand holding the gun trembled. "I know you're the one who leaked that police video to the press! You ruined my life! My acting career is over! It doesn't matter that I'm innocent. No one will ever hire me again!"

Of course. Although he was guilty, he was claiming innocence and blaming me.

Claiming and blaming. A strategy I knew all too well.

"Whoa," I said, dropping my briefcase and holding up my hands defensively. My heart pounded so hard I could hear it in my ears. "You don't want to do this. This parking lot has security cameras. Everything you do is being recorded. You don't want to get into more trouble. If you shoot me, there will be no doubt about your guilt. Do yourself a favor and put the gun down."

Out of the corner of my eye, I saw a young black man stooping behind a car and frantically dialing his cell phone, probably calling 911. I was careful not to glance his way; I didn't want to put him in danger by letting Davin know he was there.

Davin's lips snarled. "My life is over anyway."

I didn't think he would pull the trigger. I thought he was just trying to scare me, and he was doing a terrific job of it.

The bang was louder than I would have believed, ear deafening in a basement parking lot.

Everything slowed to a crawl. I could see the bullet slicing the air as it zipped toward me, but I couldn't get my body to step out of the way.

Scenes of my life flashed before my eyes like dominoes tipping over.

I'd bashed Markette in the nose . . .

Which led to me justifying bullying her . . .

Which led to a full-blown hatred of her . . .

Which led to me tossing her report card into the air . . .

Which then led to her being hit by that car and dying . . .

Which led to me regretting and desiring to make up for my sin . . .

Which led to me becoming a prosecutor of child abusers instead of the doctor my father wanted me to be...

Which led to me being shot...

And which, I knew, thanks to all the video cameras capturing the action in the parking lot, would also lead to Margie Davin being saved from her own father. A murder conviction would definitely do that.

The abuse of one girl with a brown braid and bangs was leading to freedom from far worse abuse for another.

I had prayed for a slam-dunk. It was a high price to pay, but I was getting it.

God does indeed work in mysterious ways.

It was worth it, I thought, as the bullet penetrated my chest. *It was worth even this. Lord Jesus, I give You my life.*

You know how on TV shows, when someone is shot, that person immediately crumples to the ground and lies there bleeding but not making a sound?

Not me. I stood there for a moment, screaming. The pain was agonizing; blood was seeping over my white blouse.

Davin, wide-eyed in surprise at what he had done, dropped the gun and fled. I knew, in the back of my mind, that he would be caught. Someone with a face that famous would not get away.

Then I crashed to my knees.

The man I'd seen on the phone dashed over. He mouthed some words at me, but my ears were ringing so badly from the gunshot that I couldn't hear any of it. He laid me down, whipped off his jacket, and applied pressure to the wound.

I tasted blood, and I realized a line of it was oozing out of my mouth. *It must have hit my lung*, I thought. My breathing became labored; dizziness swam through my brain.

The man's head hovered over mine, mouthing soundless words. The pain faded, and he was replaced by a familiar face.

"Markette," I whispered.

Her name was my last word on Earth.

She grasped my hands. "I'm here. Jesus sent me to get you."

We floated above my body. Gazing down at it, its wide eyes frozen in death, I understood I didn't need it anymore.

* * *

"I have something amazingly wonderful to show you," Markette said. We zipped through a tunnel of light into a place filled with fog. And there was Jesus, looking exactly like I'd always thought He would.

Markette said, "You'll see it when your Life Review is over." With that she was gone, leaving me alone with Jesus.

Standing by Him, while His burning Love surged through me, I turned my attention to the life I had led on Earth.

Some of this wasn't easy to watch . . . or relive. All my tormenting of Markette was there and I got to experience it from her point of view, although I saw that because I had repented and spent the rest of my life trying to make up for it, the pain of these scenes was greatly diminished.

Then there were the years of my life I'd spent as a District Attorney, gaining justice for abused children. I couldn't undo the damage they'd already experienced, but I did get to taste all their relief when they realized their abuse was over.

When the fog dissipated, I was standing on the summit of a high mountaintop. I didn't see Jesus anymore, although I could still sense His presence, which, of course, was absolutely everywhere. Markette was waiting for me, both hands holding upright one large white lily blazing with an unearthly light.

"See what I have for you," she said, handing it to me.

When my fingers touched the flower, the scene around me morphed into the interior of my old parish church. Markette, barely a teen, was sitting in one of the back pews with Jesus. He looked like a young teen, but now that I was in eternity, I recognized Him easily.

"What if," Jesus said, "God could make all kinds of good come out of your sufferings? What if your pain could help a lot of children who are in worse pain than you? Would that make it worthwhile?"

Markette frowned. "Well, yes. But that's not possible."

"Nothing is impossible for God," Jesus said. "Light can overcome darkness, but darkness cannot overcome light." He stared her in the eye, both index fingers straight up before his lips. "What if your death could help a lot of children? Would that

be worth dying for? Would you be willing to make that kind of sacrifice?"

Her lower lip trembled a bit.

"Would so many be worth dying for?" Jesus asked.

She inhaled deeply, then swallowed hard.

"Yes. That would be worth dying for."

* * *

Then I was back on the mountaintop, cradling the white lily. "Oh, Markette. God foresaw it all, didn't He? He knew your death would inspire me to fight for abused children. You offered up your life for them."

Her smile was, well, heavenly. "So did you. You offered up your *life*time for them, which, in a way was much harder. You had to choose over and over again to make the sacrifice. And look!"

She spread her arms wide, and only then did I notice the mountain and the valleys below were carpeted with thousands upon thousands of lilies blazing in every color, the bells of their petals softly chiming.

"What are all these?" I asked.

"Touch one and find out."

I reached over and cupped a white one near me. Again the scenery changed, this time to the inside of a different church. Amidst a large congregation a wedding was beginning, an organ playing Pachelbel's Canon. I recognized the groom standing near the altar—it was the little boy I had saved from the parents who had poisoned his baby food. He was all grown up, joyful tears streaming down his face as he watched his beautiful bride coming down the aisle and holding out her hand to him.

His joy was infectious; I shared in all the sweetness of his love for her.

When I let go, I was back on the mountaintop again. Curious, I brushed my palm over seven smaller lilies next to that one and discovered these were the children this couple would have.

Standing up, I gazed upon meadows of lilies stretching to the horizon. "How can there be this many?"

"You can see forever now," Markette said. "You can see beyond your life on Earth. These are the futures of the children you touched. And their children. And those children's children. And their children too, many generations till the end of the world."

The flowers nodded in a soft breeze, their sweet music and heavenly fragrance streaming among us.

"Oh, but this red one here," Markette said, pointing. "This is the one you spilled your blood for."

Crouching down, I cupped its bell, and I was in the Los Angeles Prosecutors' Office. I recognized a young woman working there: Margie Davin in her early thirties. Glancing around the room, I was so surprised by how much my old surroundings had changed. Margie was working at a computer, one which, I saw to my astonishment, had a flat-screen monitor instead of the big bulky ones I had been used to. Reading over her shoulder, I saw she was viewing witness statements from a case in 2024.

"She is so moved by your death," Markette explained when I let go, "that she becomes a lawyer too. These red ones stretching out from hers are the children she helps. And their children. And so forth. Do you see how the lilies you planted have seeded, sprouted, and spread?"

I stared at the fields in astonishment. I'd had this much of an impact? "I never would have imagined there would be so many!"

Markette said, "How great our God is Who can bring so much good out of evil."

I grasped Markette's hand and breathed in the heavenly fragrance of multitudes of blossoms.

"Thank you," I said. "Thank you for helping rescue me for this."

I had forever to visit any of the lilies I desired and taste the sweetness of their secrets.

As I stood on that mountain summit, gazing at thousands of flowers, I realized that even when I finished enjoying all of them, it would be but the tiniest beginning of my eternity.

Other Christian novels by A.J. Avila

Rain from Heaven

Nearer the Dawn

Amaranth

Cherish

Answer to a Prayer